HOT DADDY SAUCE

A HOT SINGLE DAD ROMANCE #1

ANGEL DEVLIN

TRACY LORRAINE

A NOTE

Hot Daddy Sauce is written in British English and contains British spelling and grammar. This may appear incorrect to some readers when compared to US English books.

1

JENSON

MY FINGERS WRAP around the fabric hanging by the window, but movement outside has me stalling. The house next door (I live in a semi-detached and our houses are joined) has been sitting empty for the past few weeks since the owners were killed in a hit and run. It might be a little rundown but that doesn't mean it wouldn't be the perfect target for kids to come and ransack the place like they seem to do for shits and giggles these days.

I wait to see if I need to be concerned, but when the person walks back to where they just were my entire body freezes. A petite woman picks up a garden fork and sticks it into the ground with all her might. She doesn't look like she should be able to lift the thing let alone swing it around the way she is.

After turning some of the flowerbed over, she starts to bend. My eyes run up the length of her bare legs before hitting the rough edge of her denim shorts and my mouth waters. They're the kind of legs that would only look better wrapped around my waist. She's just about bent all the way over, my eyes locked on her arse when it happens.

"Daddy, what's wrong?"

Damn kids and their psychic powers to interrupt at exactly the wrong time. Sucking in a deep breath and trying to calm the racing of my heart, I turn towards my little girl.

My breathing falters for another reason altogether when I take her in, snuggled under her duvet with her arm wrapped around her favourite teddy bear tightly.

"It's nothing, sweetheart. Just a bird in next door's garden that caught my attention." I cringe at my own words. It wasn't meant to come out quite like that.

"Can I see?" She goes to get out of bed, but I quickly dash over and drop to my knees beside her, pulling the book I read her every night from the bedside table.

"It flew away, baby. Now lie back, it's time for you to get some sleep."

"But, Daddy." Her sweet little voice pulls at my heartstrings and she knows it. She gets away with murder. I know I'm too easy on her but it's hard when I feel like I constantly need to make up for her lack of a mother figure.

"Don't 'but Daddy' me. You've already stayed up longer than you should watching the TV. You need to sleep and I've got work to do."

"I want to watch you cook." Her pleading eyes almost break me but knowing how much I need to do has me opening her princess book and reading the words I know off by heart. Thankfully it's exactly what she needs and only a few minutes after snuggling down, her eyes start to fall closed and her breathing evens out. I don't even get to the end of the book.

Closing it, I place it back on the bedside table and quietly stand, not taking my eyes off my daughter for a second. She's by far the best thing that ever happened to me. And like I do every time I look at how beautiful she is, appreciate how smart she is, I wonder how it couldn't possibly have been enough for her mother. I couldn't walk away and live my life without her if someone paid me. I guess it just goes to prove why I never should have married my ex in the first place. The warning signs were there but I ignored them, stupidly thinking she'd fall into her role as wife and eventually one day mother naturally. Sadly, that never happened and here I am, a single dad to the most precious gift anyone could have given me.

Flicking her light off and pulling the door closed, I can't help myself and my feet move me towards the window without instruction from my brain.

She's still digging, bending over to pull the overgrown weeds out. My cock swells as I stare at her arse, the fabric of her shorts doing very little to hide what's beneath.

Standing once again, she turns and forces the fork into the grass. Her hand lifts to brush some of her blonde hair from her forehead and she reaches for a glass of water. Tipping it to her lips, I follow the movement of her neck as she swallows and run my eyes down to her breasts. My mouth drops a little; they're huge for her tiny body and barely contained by the tight white vest she's wearing.

I shamelessly rub my cock over the fabric of my shorts, feeling it growing with need. It's been too long since he saw any action and whoever this is next door is giving him ideas.

My eyes drop, run over her tiny waist and to the

curves of her hips. Her size might make her look young, but her curves show she's all woman.

Moving to put the now empty glass down, I lean into the window a little more to keep my eyes on her. But she steps away, I guess towards the house. In my need to follow my body moves, my forehead slamming against the glass.

"Ow, fuck," I complain, pulling back and rubbing the sore spot. I guess that's what I get for perving on the girl next door.

THE WILLPOWER it took to keep away from the windows last night was impressive. No matter what I did in an attempt to distract myself, my mind kept wandering back to her full breasts and pert little arse.

"Daddy, can we have pancakes?" Amelia asks from her seat at the breakfast bar where she was busy with her colouring book.

Shaking thoughts of the woman next door from my head, I turn towards my daughter. "You had pancakes yesterday. I was going to do beans on toast."

Her face drops with disappointment and it hits

me exactly where she intends. "Please, Daddy. They're my favourite."

"Okay, but tomorrow you're having beans."

"Okay," she sings but I can already picture us having this exact same conversation tomorrow morning.

I'm just sliding the first pancake onto Amelia's plate when there's a crash and squeal from outside.

She jumps down from her stool at the same time I turn off the hob and turn towards the open French doors.

"Who was that?" Amelia asks as I head towards the gate at the side of our house.

"Next door, I think."

I expect her to tell me that can't be the case because the house is empty, but to my surprise she accepts my answer and follows me. Obviously too keen to find out what's going on.

I spot her the second we round the hedge that surrounds the property next door. She's sitting on the stone driveway, inspecting her knee as a small trail of blood runs down her shin. Behind her lies the ladder she must have fallen off and a pair of garden shears.

"Shit," the woman cries in fright, the crunching stones under my feet announcing our arrival. Her eyes widen as she takes me in, but they soon drop to

6

Amelia who's hiding behind me. "Fuck, I didn't mean to... crap."

"It's okay. Daddy says naughty words all the time," Amelia pipes up, stepping around me and walking towards the woman on the floor. "Did you fall over?"

"I did," she confirms, her eyes softening as she watches Amelia approach her. I'm grateful she's distracted because it means she won't see me shamelessly staring at her cleavage.

I really need to get laid.

"My daddy can clean it. He's really gentle. It never hurts when he cleans my cuts. We've even got princess plasters; they have magic powers to make it all better."

"Is that right?"

My skin tingles, forcing me to look up, knowing I've been caught ogling her while she's down.

"Uh... yeah... special powers," I mutter like an imbecile.

"Daddy, are you going to help?" I don't need to look at Amelia to know she's standing with her hands on her hips, her lips curled into a pout.

"Yeah, of course." Walking over, I reach my hand out to help pull the woman from the ground. She slides her tiny hand into mine and I almost let go the second an electric spark shoots up my arm. My eyes find her blue ones. They're narrowed at me in confusion making me wonder if she felt that too.

"Ready?" She nods slightly and I tug her up from the ground. I stand back as she brushes herself off, trying desperately hard not to follow her hands as they move around her body but failing miserably. "Are you okay?"

"I think so, just this," she says, pointing towards her knee which is now really starting to bleed. "I guess it's my own fault for leaning too far over trying to trim this hedge. I just wanted it done before it got too hot."

"It has been hot around here recently." *What the fuck is wrong with me? I sound like a horny teenage boy.* Her eyebrow lifts in amusement, forcing me to make an even bigger dick of myself. "You know, with the heatwave and all."

"Sure. I'm Leah, by the way."

"Aw, that's a pretty name. I'm Amelia and this is my daddy." Amelia's excited to have someone new to chat to and she smiles at the woman.

"It's nice to meet you, Amelia. You have a pretty name too. I really like the bow in your hair." Amelia beams at her praise and my heart twists in my chest reminding me how much she must miss out on without her mother about.

"And your daddy's name is...?" she trails off, her head tipping back so she can meet my eyes.

"Jenson. Jenson Hale."

"Nice to meet you, Jenson Hale. I'm Leah Ward." She turns and bends over to pick up the ladder and a low moan rumbles up my throat. I cough to try to cover it, but once she's upright again with the ladder in her hand she turns to me, a smirk playing on her lips.

"Daddy's making me pancakes. You should come and have some. He can clean your knee too."

"Oh... uh... I'm not..."

"You're more than welcome. And you really should get that cleaned in case you've got something in it."

"Y- yeah, I guess." She looks down to her bloody knee and then to Amelia who's practically bouncing with excitement.

"If you're a good girl, Daddy might let you have Nutella on your pancakes."

Leah's amused and slightly heated eyes turn to me. "Is that right? You'd better lead the way then."

I allow them to walk ahead of me. I try to tell myself that it's because I'm a gentleman, but really it's so I can see how Leah's arse swings in those sinfully small shorts. And fuck me if it isn't the best sight I've seen in a long time.

I knew the couple next door had a grown-up daughter, they'd mentioned her a couple of times in passing, but too focused on my own issues, I never really paid any attention to any details they might have given me. Suddenly, I wished I'd made the effort to listen, because now I want to know everything, but most importantly how old she is, because while my body is screaming at me to take what I need, my head is in a much more sensible place telling me that she's way too young for me.

2

LEAH

SO MUCH FOR my plan to get in this house, do what needs doing and get out again as fast as is humanly possible. The truth is that this home is full of my parents, their essence, and I'm here stripping it away so that some new family can move in and make happy memories. As I clear the place, it takes a piece of my soul each time.

Just a month ago, I had a mum and dad. The amount of times I was at college and I saw their names flash on my mobile phone screen and I ignored it because I couldn't be bothered to talk to them... now I'd do anything to hear their voices. Wiped out in the blink of an eye in a hit and run. The driver on drugs has shown no remorse, just feeble excuses that he can't remember what happened.

I'll never forget. The police at my door asking if they could come in and then telling me something that would change my life forever.

And now I'm sitting at a kitchen table in the house next door while a little girl tells me her life story and her dad walks towards me with a first aid kit.

What's worse is that I'm perfectly capable of cleaning my own wound and putting a plaster on it, but I'm so going to let him do it, because my god, he's sexy as all hell, and my life has to have some good in it.

I look at the tall sex god walking towards me. If I'd known he lived next door, I'd have visited more often. He must be six foot tall. His dark blonde hair is shaved at the sides. I want to stroke my fingers on it to feel the stubble. He has sculpted cheekbones; a strong nose; and soft, pink lips. My eyes travel down taking in his beard. I bet that would tickle...

"Okay, swing your legs around to me, so I can get to that cut."

My breath hitches at his gruff tone. God, he can command me any day. I do as he asks.

Jenson drops down to his knees. Oh boy...

He dips the cotton wool in the bowl of warm water, and then his head tips up towards me, his hazel eyes meeting my own blues.

"This might hurt a bit."

Fuck, my mind had gone to him being between my legs and apologising for his mammoth dick, but no, as the warm water bathes my cut and I wince, I'm reminded that boringly he really is just cleaning my wound.

"Daddy, you're getting Leah all wet." Amelia jumps off her stool and runs off. She comes back over with a towel and hands it to him.

"Erm, yeah, sorry about that." He drops the used cotton wool in the bowl and pats at my leg gently.

"It's not a problem. I'll soon dry off in this heat anyway. Not like yesterday. I was outside and got caught in a downpour. I was soaking wet then."

Leah, shut the fuck up about being wet, I tell myself, while trying not to think about the fact that I am indeed soaking wet, my knickers damp, because of the ministrations of this stranger on my knee. Turned on by first aid. Whatever next? I can tell it's been a while since someone paid my body any attention.

"Okay, it's clean. Now I'll just put a plaster on."

"No, Daddy, Leah needs the magic cream."

Amelia turns to me. "Daddy rubs it on very, very carefully so it doesn't hurt too much and do you like pink or purple best because I like you and so you can have one of my princess plasters. Then when you've had your pancakes, I can show you my bedroom because that's got princesses everywhere."

"I must apologise. My daughter is princess mad." Jenson looks into his daughter's eyes. With him being on his knees, I can see the look of love that passes between them. "Baby girl, when we've had pancakes, Leah will have to go back because she was busy in the garden, wasn't she?"

Amelia's expression sinks with disappointment and her shoulders slump. "Okay, Daddy." She turns to me. "You just look like one of my princesses. I called her Sophie, but now I'm going to change her name to Leah. Princess Leah."

I see Jenson's mouth curl up at the corner at this. Obviously the Star Wars reference isn't lost on him even if my name isn't spelled or sounds exactly that way. God, now my mind is imagining my hair curled up like Princess Leia's and some kind of kinky role play. I really need to get laid and soon.

I note Jenson's hesitation before he picks out the tube of Savlon from his first aid kit, unscrews the lid and then pushes out a small bit of cream. He then shakes his head and offers it to me. "Do you want to do this?"

"No, Daddy. Don't be silly. The magic is in your fingers. How is Leah's knee going to get better without the magic?" She eye rolls him, which is entirely adorable. Her dark blonde, curly hair shakes around her shoulders. Her eyes are the exact colour of her dad's.

"Well, if your daddy's fingers are magic then I'd better let him put the cream on." I'm openly smirking now. It goes completely over Amelia's head, but there's a faint blush to her father's cheeks. He mouths, "Oh my god," at me, followed by, "sorry."

Then he begins to rub the cream onto my graze.

"Can you feel the magic?" Amelia says wide-eyed, looking at me eagerly.

"I really, really can. Amelia, your daddy really does have magic fingers." I say, watching as Jenson's face creases up with awkwardness.

"Amelia. Why don't you go and fetch that princess doll you wanted to show Leah?" Jenson says.

"Oh, good idea. I'll be right back, Leah. Don't go anywhere." She goes running off and I hear her little footsteps pad upstairs. The minute she's out of the room, Jenson stops rubbing at my knee and sits back groaning.

"I am so sorry. This is the most awkward encounter I've had with a female in a long time."

That's it, I'm gone. I laugh loudly, and I welcome it because it's the first joy I've felt in weeks. "Now, I'm not going to complain about your magic fingers."

He holds a hand over his eyes peeping through them. "Stop, please. I'm so embarrassed." He hands me a plaster. Quick, put this on. Sorry but it has to be a princess one; you're not going to get away with anything less."

"You mean I have to place this on myself? No more magic fingers?" I pout at him.

"Nope, I have to pace myself, or I'll lose my magic touch." He winks and this time it's my turn to feel a little heat at my cheeks. Is this just banter to break an awkward moment or is he actually flirting with me?

I don't get time to think on it any further as a Disney Cinderella doll is more or less thrown at me. "See, it's Cinderella, but I like to rename them and make my own stories for them, so this was Princess Sophie, but now she's Princess Leah, and look she's hurt herself in the garden." Amelia points to where she's drawn a red graze on the doll's knee with what looks like felt-tip pen. "Now the prince can make the princess better later." she tells me. "Oh, great, you have the princess plaster on. You'll be better in no time, won't she, Daddy?" Her little voice rambles on at a hundred miles an hour. "Now it's time for pancakes. Do you want raspberry sauce and chocolate sprinkles?"

"Erm, what else is there?"

"Sugar, lemon juice, chocolate sauce, orange juice, maple syrup. I have to keep a supply of everything in with this young lady. Her tastes can be very demanding."

"I'll have sugar and lemon juice on mine please."

"Coming right up. Amelia?"

"Raspberry sauce done as a smiley face please, and chocolate sprinkle eyebrows and a moustache." She giggles. "Daddy makes the best faces on pancakes. He's so funny. Did your daddy make you pancakes when you were a little girl?"

And just like that I feel sliced in two. Like an ice-cold wind has hit my throat on a cross-country run, I gasp. My hands going to my mouth.

"Shoot, I'm so sorry." Jenson asks.

I breathe deeply. *You're okay, Leah*, I tell myself. *It will pass.*

"What's the matter?" Amelia looks panicked.

17

"My cut stung a little." I lie. "But it's okay now."

I watch as she scrambles onto her chair at the table, sitting next to me.

"My daddy used to make me runny eggs with soldiers. Have you had those?"

Amelia's head nods up and down eagerly. "Oh yes, I love those. Come tomorrow and Daddy can make us them."

"I might be busy tomorrow..." I say, noting the disappointment hit her features once more.

Pancakes are placed in front of me and Jenson offers me a coffee to go with it. I'd not had breakfast this morning and I hadn't realised just how hungry I'd become. The pancakes are delicious: thin, crispy, and just the right amount of sweet and sour. I clear my plate in no time and then find yet another placed on my plate. I manage three before I shake my head at Jenson's offer of another.

"Wow, I think I'm going to burst." I say rubbing at my stomach. I note Jenson's eyes linger at my breasts for a second. Yeah, my ample rack looks like it could burst from my top any time. I might be short, but I'm stacked.

Finishing up my coffee, I clamber off my seat. "Well, thanks for the breakfast, guys, and for treating my poorly knee. I'd better get back to work now. I have some men coming over later to help clear the house and do some repairs."

"So, are you moving in?" Jenson asks.

I shake my head. "No, I'm getting the place ready for sale. It needs a little updating and then I can get it on the market." I don't explain about the debt I'd found my parents had got themselves in unknown to me. How they'd been ripped off by a scam. Now I needed to get the best price for the house to clear the debt because they'd no other money left to cover anything. I'd be lucky to walk away with a penny after all this; but selling the house would draw a line under it all. Then I could try to move on with my life.

"Well, if there's anything I can do to help?" Jenson says. It's the kind of empty gesture people make to you when someone has died. I've heard it aplenty the last few weeks and yet with Jenson, I feel it's a genuine offer, that if I said right now that I needed the lawn mowing, he'd be there. But he has his little girl to take care of. I don't know where her mum is, maybe at work, but I don't see a ring on his finger.

"Thanks, but I'll let you get on." I say. "Maybe I'll meet Mrs Hale sometime?"

God, I can't help myself.

"Oh no." Amelia says. "Mummy doesn't live here. She fucked off to New York, didn't she, Daddy?"

I watch as Jenson wipes his palms down his face and once more peers through his fingers at me with a look of horror.

I place my own hand over my mouth stifling the giggle that threatens to unleash itself. I also note my inward pleasure at the fact that Jenson Hale is a hot single daddy. Suddenly, despite the shit going on in my life, there seems to be a rainbow appearing between the clouds. A six-foot muscular rainbow named Jenson.

3

_____

JENSON

I WATCH her arse sway as she walks through the French doors and back in the direction of her parents' house.

My mind drifts back over our short time together. Her reaction to me was impossible to miss. The catching of her breath when I first touched her, the darkening of her blue eyes and the unmissable tightening of her nipples that had my imagination running wild. With her soft floral scent surrounding me, I could almost imagine what it might be like to strip her out of the few clothes she was wearing and run my hands over more than just her grazed knee.

"Daddy, do you have to go to work today?" Amelia's words barely register, my mind still in the gutter.

"Huh?"

"Are you going to work today?" she repeats slowly like I might be hard of hearing.

"Oh, yeah. Auntie Kaylie will be here soon."

"Aww, but I thought you were going to take me swimming."

"Not today, baby." And definitely not when my cock's still feeling the effects Leah had on it. "Maybe at the weekend."

Her soft pink lips curl into a pout and she lets out a sigh. It only lasts two seconds at best before she jumps up in excitement. "Can we invite Leah?"

"Erm, I'm not sure she has time for swimming dates with you, madam."

"But... can you at least ask?"

I should say no, it would be the most sensible thing to do, but as her hazel eyes bore into mine, I don't have it in me. "We can ask." Her little face lights up and her fists clench as she hisses a little 'yes' in celebration.

The image of Leah in an itsy bitsy bikini pops into my head and I will it to go back down. It's never going to happen.

"Can you go and get your teeth brushed please so you're ready for Auntie Kaylie?"

"Okay, Daddy." She skips out of the room with

her princess doll swinging from her hand and my heart aches.

Seeing her with Leah this morning just goes to prove how much she needs a mother. My sister does a great job babysitting whenever I need her to, but it's not the same thing as having a female in the house. I hate to think I'm letting Amelia down in some way when my sole purpose in life right now is to make her happy.

With Amelia happily playing in her room, I quickly walk into mine to change ready to head into work. I trained as a chef straight from school. Cooking was the only thing I've ever wanted to do. I remember begging my mum and dad for a little play kitchen when I was a kid and I've been obsessed ever since. The Grill was my first job as head chef. I was younger than most of the other guys and a lot of them made it very clear how they felt about a 'kid' coming in above them, but thankfully my skill spoke for itself and they soon accepted my position. Fast forward a few years and The Grill is now called InHale and I'm no longer the head chef but the owner. When my old boss told me about his plans to retire, I saw it as a sign and after a good few meetings at the bank, along with some early inheritance from my parents, I was able to achieve my dream. It's been hard work, really fucking hard work, but it's been totally worth it. Although it meant that I was essentially hanging up my chef's hat, it also meant that I could leave behind the unsociable hours and be around for Amelia. When she was first born, I'd miss putting her to bed at night and still be sleeping when she woke first thing in the morning. I hated it. But now, being the boss means that I can be much more flexible. I've employees who I trust to keep the place going in my absence, so not only do I have a job I love and pays well, but I'm also able to spend as much time with my daughter as possible.

I'm just buttoning up my shirt when the doorbell rings throughout the house.

"Auntie Kay's here," Amelia squeals before the sound of her little feet thundering down the stairs fills my ears. She really loves my sister, much to Kaylie's delight. While I spent my time pretending to make meals out of plastic food, Kaylie was nurturing her dolls and nothing's really changed for either of us. She's now a primary school teacher so while she seems to be forever single with no chance of a family of her own anytime soon, she still manages to surround herself with kids most of the time.

"Mornin', Kay," I say when I find her barely

inside the house with Amelia chatting away about something she saw on TV last night.

"Will you at least allow Auntie Kaylie past the door before you make her ears bleed?"

"Daddy," Amelia huffs, hands on her hips and eyes narrowed in my direction. "Auntie Kay was the one who asked me about it."

"Okay, sorry," I say, backing towards the kitchen with my hands up in defeat.

The sounds of them chatting filters through to me as I collect up all the samples I made last night. I'm currently knee deep in our autumn menu planning. The restaurant has always done well, but since we had a very well-respected critic give us rave reviews in the earlier part of the year things have gone from strength to strength. However, menu planning that I used to find enjoyable has suddenly turned into something full of stress and pressure. We've now got a reputation and I'd like to keep it for the foreseeable future.

"So... how are things?" my sister asks, walking in and immediately going for the coffee machine.

"Things are... good." My words falter slightly as I'm reminded just how good things were only this morning while I had my hands on the girl next door.

"I can't believe you let her have pancakes for breakfast again," Kaylie scolds like I'm the child.

"What? They're her favourite and it's the holidays. Mum used to make us pancakes in the holidays."

"She'd also insist we had fruit with them."

"And how do you know Amelia didn't?"

"Because she already told me she had raspberry sauce and chocolate sprinkles."

"Remind me to be this annoying when you have a child of your own."

"Chance would be a fine thing," she grumbles, pulling the fridge open to find the milk.

"It'll happen, Kay. You've just got to wait for the right guy to fall into your lap."

"Yeah that plan's not really working out for me, if I'm being honest."

"It'll happen," I say again, confident that there's someone out there for her. As much as I love her spending all her spare time here babysitting, I hate to stop her living her own life. "Why don't you go out this weekend?"

"Don't you need me to look after Amelia Friday and Saturday night?"

"I'll sort something." I've no idea how but I need to start thinking about her life as well as mine.

"Are you sure?" I can see in her eyes that she wants me to say no, that really she'd rather be here hiding than out trying to find a guy, but I won't allow it.

"Yes, positive. Call up the girls and get a wild weekend planned."

"I'm not sure I've ever had a wild weekend in my life."

"Well there's no time like the present. If you need a table to kick off the night, let me know."

"Will do."

"I'll only be a few hours," I say, picking up the pile of tubs and paperwork from the counter.

"Let me take those." Kaylie takes the files from the top and follows me towards the door.

"Thank you." Turning towards my sister, I take the files from her hands and place them in the boot along with the tubs. I'm just shutting it when a van pulls up on next door's drive and a guy gets out. I watch as he goes to knock, but the door's pulled open before he gets a chance. Leah's still in the skin-tight vest and almost non-existent shorts. Even from behind I see his head drop to check her out. My blood boils and an unwelcome feeling that I don't want to acknowledge twists my stomach. I've spent less than an hour with her, there's no way I should be feeling like this knowing she's about to let a man into her house.

Just before she goes to step back to allow him to pass her, our eyes connect over his shoulder. Electricity like I remember all too well from this morning passes between us and I feel it all the way down to my cock. My fists clench as I fight the need to go over and ensure that whoever he is keeps his hands to himself. My teeth grind as she smiles at me and closes the front door.

"Is everything okay?" my sister asks sceptically.

"Perfect," I seethe through gritted teeth.

"Your new neighbour's hot."

Turning towards her my chin drops. "Maybe that's why you don't have a man, if you spend your time checking out girls?"

Jutting one hip out, her eyebrow quirks up. "Just making an observation in case you hadn't noticed. I'm not the only one standing here who'd benefit from a little attention from the opposite sex."

"I'm not standing here having a conversation with you that involves the word sex. I've got work to do."

"Don't you always."

I go to respond but deciding it's pointless, I head for the driver's door instead. I start the engine and begin backing off the drive as my sister heads towards the house. Reversing off, I tell myself to keep my head down, but just as I put the car into drive my eyes find their way to Leah's large bay window. I immediately find her staring right back at me. The man she let inside is standing in front of her talking away but there's no way she's listening to him. The moment she realises I caught her, she drags her eyes away, but not before I catch the blush that covers her cheeks.

My fingers tighten around the wheel as I fight an urge to pull back on the drive, march into her house and take exactly what I need.

Sucking in a large breath, I pull my eyes away and slam my foot down, ensuring my car takes me away from temptation as fast as possible.

4

LEAH

TRYING to garden with an injured knee is not fun. I decide to abandon thoughts of weeding flowerbeds given I'd need to be on my knees or bending over which would hurt my neck. Instead I'll start a bit of painting. Painting my room will also be painful but for an entirely different reason. My mum had this room decorated in my favourite colours of cerise and baby pinks. Today I'm going to use magnolia to wipe away all traces of my personality from my bedroom while Carl continues plastering the walls of the living room, now the years of wallpaper have been stripped from them.

I throw myself on my bed and sigh. Looking around, I try to fix my room into my memory bank. Except instead thoughts of the hot daddy next door come into my mind. Between my thighs I feel my knickers soak once more as I think about his fingers stroking my knee.

Closing my eyes, I take my own fingers and stroke at my knee just as he did, imagining it's his own. God, I'm a sad cow, but I'm also mega turned on now and seeing it's a rare time at the moment with no one else in the house, I intend to make the most of it. My fingers become Jenson's and they trail up my thighs. In my fantasies Amelia has gone to stay with mummy and we are definitely home alone.

Dipping my fingers to my sweet spot, I groan as I flick my fingertip at my nub. Self-love is usually just a means to an end for me, but now, imagining Jenson touching me intimately, I am on fire. My fingertips sweep over my clit again and again and then I take two fingers of my other hand and push them inside me, now imagining Jenson's throbbing cock pushing in deep. Before long I'm bucking over my fingers as my body trembles with an explosive orgasm.

And then my face flushes as guilt hits about what I've just done. How will I look him in the face now? I rush to the bathroom and shower as if I can wash off all trace of my masturbation session. The water makes my princess plaster come loose and fall into the shower tray and makes me feel even guiltier.

I dry myself off quickly and get dressed as the plasterer will be back again soon and then heading to the kitchen I make myself a coffee. Despite my recent orgasm, a feeling of general frustration seems to have seeped into my bones. Hearing voices outside, I spy through the edge of my curtain and see Jenson with another woman. Fuck. With him saying he had an ex-wife, I'd presumed he was single. My stomach suddenly feels lined with lead and if I didn't want to risk a broken toe, I'd probably kick the wall. They are carrying tubs and files to his car and I wonder what they are. The plasterer's van turns onto the street and I get excited that I have an excuse to get to the door, an opportunity to say hi to Jenson again.

What about the woman? Sure she'll be impressed if you start waving and simpering at her man. God, my inner thoughts are a party pooper.

I quickly run my hands through my hair like a sad bitch before opening the door to let Carl in. As I greet him and step back to let him pass, my eyes meet Jenson's. His gaze is steely and focused and I can't work out his facial expression. He seems a little pissed with me, but I've not done anything. Oh, he's probably off to work and late, stressed. I need to stop being so paranoid all the time. I'd always been confident and scared of nothing until my parents unexpected deaths. Now I feel constantly on edge, wondering if anything else wants to turn my life upside down.

I follow Carl into the living room, and I know he's chatting away to me but I'm in the window looking at Jenson again as he bids goodbye to the mystery woman and drives off. She must be important because she's looking after Amelia and I know already from one meeting that Jenson would not allow just anyone to care for his daughter.

"Earth calling Leah."

I turn and stare at Carl, with a no doubt vacant expression on my face.

"God, I'm so sorry, Carl." I lift up my coffee mug. "I'm half dead today, hence this is my third cup. You fancy one?"

"I'm guessing you mean a coffee?" Carl quips. He's a typical workman, with a pleasant demeanour and a cheeky bluster about him. His eyes have looked me up and down twice already today but hell, he's male, and I know my clothes are scanty, but it's so hot weather wise and doing physical work makes it even worse. Soon, Carl will remove his t-shirt and I'll be checking out those toned abs of his so I can't complain he checks me out too. Tall, with sandy, wavy hair and green eyes, Carl is a good looking guy, but when I look at him there's no connection. Not like I had with Jenson.

God, will you stop mooning about Jenson, it's pathetic. He has a girlfriend and Carl's single. Flirt with Carl.

But I can't. Jenson's hazel gaze meeting mine is on repeat in my mind.

I spend the rest of the morning emptying my bedroom into boxes: some things to keep, some for charity, some for the bin. Once it's painted, I will live in my personality-free bedroom until it becomes someone else's. I have all the neutral new bedding purchased along with matching curtains. A blank slate for someone else.

From then on it's masking tape everywhere and by the time lunchtime comes around I'm a sweaty heap. Carl has brought lunch, so I just make him another drink, and I take my own sandwich and glass of water into the garden.

My parents' back garden is long with a decking area at the top with a table and chairs and then it leads down to a grassed area. At the bottom is a glass greenhouse next to my father's vegetable patch. I've been watering everything that was left in there but that's been it. I guess really I should harvest any veg that's ready, but I've been existing on pizza and takeaways, evidenced by the extra few pounds on my tits and arse. It's hard to cook for one. Maybe I could invite Jenson and Amelia around for a meal? Except, I can barely cook. Wandering down to the veg patch, I try to work out what's in there. Little stringy bean things, tomatoes, cucumbers that are so huge they look obscene, and a row of chillis. What the heck was my dad intending to do with that many? Finding a clean large plant pot in the greenhouse, I start taking off everything that seems ready. I'll take a load of veg around next door later tonight as a thank you for them caring for me and feeding me this morning and I'll try to find out who the woman is like the sad bitch I am.

My bedroom looks over the back garden and once I'm back there after my garden foraging and eating my lunch, I emulsion a wall and then peer out nosying as I watch Amelia running around her garden dressed as a princess. Christ, she must be roasting hot in that costume. Sure enough, the woman comes out and inflates a paddling pool, putting the hose in it to fill it and then changes Amelia into a swimsuit and lathers her in suntan lotion. They look so comfortable together. This woman has clearly been in Amelia's life for a long time. She's slim and pretty, with light-brown curly hair. Dressed in a long yellow sundress with a daisy design on it, she looks the epitome of effortless summer glamour. Her feet are encased in gold sandals. As she walks, her buttoned up sundress reveals a hint of shapely calf. Goddamn it. I take my frustrations out on the next wall, getting more paint on my body, face, and in my hair as I smack the roller onto the plaster and push it up and down. I turn on the radio to drown out the sounds of the two of them enjoying themselves in the garden.

"I'M DONE for the day, darlin'." I pivot to find Carl standing in the doorway. "Jesus, you look like you got more paint on yourself than the wall." He sniggers, once more appraising my body, although this time it's amusement not lust reflected in his features.

I grin back at him. "Yep, but the job's almost done, so it's worth it. Emulsion washes off easily enough."

"True. So anyway, the living room is all done. I'll be back tomorrow for the kitchen. We're getting there, Leah. The weather will help loads with drying the walls, but leave the windows open and my industrial fans on okay?"

I salute him and a spray of paint flows out in his general direction. Thank God for distance between us, and old curtains covering my carpet. Once these walls have another coat of paint later on, I can get cleared up and the carpet cleaned and this room will be done.

I hear the door close and breathe out a huge exhale with relief that once more it's just me in the house. Time for another coffee break, then to get the second coat of paint on, and then another shower and another takeaway. I have no energy for cooking tonight. I have barely enough to paint again. The heat and the effort are wiping me out.

So it's funny later after my takeaway that I suddenly have enough energy to pop next door with my now bagged up veggies. Given how sophisticated the woman next door looked, I put on a mint-coloured tea-dress that my mother made me buy for a wedding reception, along with a pair of grey kitten heels. I straighten my hair and add a light dusting of make-up. I don't want to appear like I'm trying too hard. I watched the woman leave earlier so I know there are only the two of them in the house now. Grabbing my plastic bag full of veg, I open my door, removing the key and putting it in my little grey shoulder bag and then I walk down my path, across the front, and up their path.

With one last smooth of my hair and my dress, I ring the doorbell.

I hear an, "Amelia, come back. What have I told you about safety? Adults answer the door, not six-year-olds." A curtain pulls back and Jenson's gaze meets mine through the window. I smile and my smile is returned. Then a little body pushes past him and Amelia is waving and grinning through the window and I notice she has a gap at the middle of her top row of teeth where this morning there was none.

They disappear from the window and there's a fiddling of a key in the lock and then the door opens and he's standing in front of me. He's dressed in an open white shirt, and I find it quite hard not to pass out from sheer lust from where I'm standing. I can see a six-pack and oh my fucking god there's the 'v' running into his low-slung jeans. This shouldn't be allowed. God, that lucky bitch who just left. *Please let her just be a childminder*, I beg to every deity I know.

"Hey." I hold up the bag. "So, my dad used to be a keen gardener and I've rescued some veg from the patch. There's far too much for me, and to be honest, I can barely cook, so can you use any of this?" I hand over the bag.

"You don't need to cook. My daddy's a chef. He can cook all your dinners, can't you, Daddy?" Amelia jumps up and down excitedly. "What's in the bag, Daddy? Show me."

He looks at me and at Amelia and back again. "I have a little budding chef of my own."

"Ah, right. I brought these to the right place then."

"Tomatoes, cumber. What are those little red things, Daddy? Are they baby peppers?"

"They're chillis, sweetpea. And they are spicy hot. You have to be careful with cutting and handling those so for now they are just for me to use okay? You stick with the tomatoes." He passes a small cherry one to her and she stuffs it in her mouth. "That's so delicious. I think that's the best tomato I ever tasted. Another, Daddy, another."

He lifts up a pepper and stares at it. "Wow, a Bird's Eye chilli," he says. I look at him, feeling a crease come to my brow.

"Bird's Eye? Like the people who make fish fingers?"

He guffaws with laughter. "No, that's the name

of the variety. It originated in Thailand, Cambodia, places like that; but it's used around the world in cuisine now. They're called Bird's Eye because of their roundish shape and the fact that birds spread them.

"Oh." I reply feeling stupid.

"I like your dress." Amelia says. "Does it twirl?"

"Er, I'm not sure." I reply honestly, bearing in mind I never got up to dance at the wedding reception because the DJ insisted on playing shit like The Birdie Song all night.

"Well, try please."

"Amelia, stop being bossy."

"It's okay." I tell her dad. "I'll try it."

So I swirl around and sure enough the dress twirls and then the summer breeze gets behind it and the next thing I know, I've flashed my thong at the pair of them.

"I can see your bum!" Amelia giggles.

I want to die.

5

JENSON

WHEN THE DOORBELL rings I'm expecting it to be some irritating salesman at the other side that we seem to be inundated with at the moment. I panic when I see Amelia rush towards the door because those men could be anyone. I hate that I get so paranoid, but I can't help it, my protective nature knows no bounds when it comes to my daughter. What I'm not expecting when I pull the curtain back to reveal who's standing at our front door is Leah. Only, she doesn't look a bit like I remember because gone are the tiny gardening clothes she was barely covered by this morning, and in their place is a cute little dress which looks like something I might put Amelia in. My stomach twists as I'm reminded of how young my new next-door neighbour is and just how inappropriate my sudden crush is.

"It's Leah," Amelia squeals excitedly when she joins me at the window. "Quick, let's invite her in for Cinderella."

Amelia's gone before I get the chance to make an excuse and when I catch up with her, she's already at the front door twisting the key.

Glancing down at myself, I realise I should probably tell Amelia to wait and button up my shirt but ever hopeful that Leah might see something she likes, much like I do every time I've laid my eyes on her, I push the thought aside and pull the door wide.

My breath catches the moment my gaze lands on her. She looked beautiful through the window but being right in front of her is so much more intense. Her eyes hold mine and her lips curl up in a slightly shy smile before she holds her hand out and shows me something that gets me even more excited. A bag of veg!

I get a little overexcited about the fresh produce she's brought around for me. She can't possibly know my obsession with food from the few minutes we spent together this morning, so it's either a good guess or she needed an excuse to come back. I like to think it's the latter of the two options, but fuck knows why. I'm a single dad to a little girl who single-handedly embarrassed both of us only hours ago. Why would she risk coming back?

My obsession with the veg gets the better of me and I soon end up showing my inner food geek by relaying my detailed knowledge about the Birds Eye chilli, much to Leah's amusement.

Thankfully my daughter rescues me, but in true Amelia style she manages to cause even more embarrassment when she insists that Leah does a twirl in her dress and she ends up flashing us both with her bare arse.

The second the fabric lifts and reveals her smooth, flawless, peachy arse, my mouth waters and I find myself biting down on my bottom lip, wondering how it might feel if it was her arse. My cock swells and I feel like a fucking teenager again getting his first look at a naked woman. *It's only her arse, Jenson. Get a grip.*

"Shit... *fuck*. Oh my god, I'm so sorry. I should go. Shit. Grrr."

Leah goes to take a step back, but I take pity on her, or at least that's what I tell myself as I try to ignore the disappointment that floods me as I consider her leaving so soon.

"Wait," I call. "Would you like to come in?"

"Yes," Amelia squeals, "We're about to watch Cinderella before I have to go to bed." I don't need to look at my daughter to know the end of that sentence came with an eye roll. "Daddy can make you one of his magical hot chocolates."

The mention of chocolate seems to perk Leah back up a little, although it's not enough for her to agree.

"Oh no, I shouldn't intrude. I've got plenty to be doing."

"Are you going out?" I ask, realising that she's dressed up like she should be. "Date?"

Her cheeks flush. "Oh, no. I just... uh... my mum bought this for me so I wanted to..." she trails off and I feel awful. She's already been through enough and between the two of us we keep making it worse.

"Please, come in. Don't let that pretty dress go to waste."

"I'll go and put the DVD in." Amelia's gone before I have a chance to blink and Leah steps towards me.

"You think it's pretty?"

"Uh... yeah, I guess. I mean, it's the kind of thing that Amelia would choose, so..." I trail off feeling like a dick for comparing her sexy as sin dress to one belonging to my six-year-old.

"Riiight."

"Um… you should come in before she comes to find you."

"Sure."

Stepping back, I allow her to enter. The second she moves past me her sweet scent fills my nose and my cock threatens to go full mast behind my zip.

"I was just about to jump in the shower. I'll make the hot chocolate when I come back down."

"Isn't it a little hot for that?" Her eyes drop from mine to my bare chest for a split second and my brain misfires as I wonder what she's talking about.

"Yeah… um… I'll be back."

Fucking hell, anyone would think I've never spoken to a female before in my life. I shake my head in frustration as I climb the stairs, my balls aching with my need for release like they have been since my eyes first landed on Leah in a heap on the floor in the garden.

Turning the shower on, I twist the temperature straight to cold. I need to get myself together before I go back down and try to act like she hasn't sent my world into a tailspin. My focus needs to be my daughter and my business. I've no time to fantasising about the girl next door, her tiny denim hot pants, and her black lace thong.

Shit, shit, shit.

I don't allow myself to think about it; the second I step under the freezing cold water, I wrap my fist around my solid cock and tug. A groan rumbles up my throat but I swallow it down for fear of being heard.

I'm so worked up after having images of Leah in those damn shorts on repeat in my mind all day that it takes embarrassingly few pumps of my cock before releasing my seed into the swirling water at my feet.

My muscles relax for a beat but as soon as the thought of her sitting downstairs with Amelia enters my head, it feels like it was all for nothing. I fear nothing short of having her under me is going to fix my current situation.

Stepping out, I wrap a towel around my waist and head out to find some fresh clothes. I automatically reach for a pair of jersey shorts but when I notice my cock's already tenting the towel once again, I think better of it. That fabric shows enough at the best of times, I don't need to be walking down there—where my daughter is, I remind myself—showing off my semi.

Sounds of their joyful chatter fills the air as I descend the stairs and head towards the kitchen for Amelia's nightly treat. Leah was right, it is a bit hot for it, but Amelia insists and who am I to take that little pleasure away from her?

I make Amelia's standard mug, swirl cream around the steaming chocolate and then sprinkle a few marshmallows to finish it off before turning to grab a bottle of coffee liqueur to spike the adults' drinks with. Placing all three on a tray, I carry them through.

The sight in the living room stops me in my tracks when I get to the doorway. Amelia and Leah have made themselves a den—or knowing my daughter it's probably meant to be a castle—and they're both laid out surrounded by sofa cushions with a blanket precariously draped over the top, watching Cinderella.

My heart aches. Amelia should have someone she can do this with every day. I thought I hated her mother when she first left, but now understanding everything Amelia is missing out on because of her mother's selfish actions makes me hate her even more. I've no idea how I didn't see it prior to her falling pregnant. Not that it would make a difference because I can't regret any of it. I've got the most incredible daughter and right now, that's all that matters.

I step a little into the room and their heads come

into view. I can't help the laugh that falls from my lips when I find them both wearing tiaras and Amelia with one of her dress up dresses over the top of her pyjamas.

"Oh the hot chocolate's here. You're going to love it, Leah. Daddy makes it perfect."

Leah glances up at me. My heart pounds the second our eyes connect and I swear hers darken as our contact holds.

"Well, I can't wait for a taste then."

The ache I'm becoming used to when I'm around her starts up and the tray trembles in my hands.

Thankfully, the sight of Amelia scrambling from their makeshift castle catches my eye and she races over to take her mug.

Leah is slightly more elegant as she crawls from beneath the blanket, although it doesn't mean I don't get a great shot straight down the front of her dress.

"Hmmm... smells incredible," she all but moans when she gets to me and takes the closest mug.

"I made yours extra special," I say with a wink.

"Well, I can't wait to experience it. Thank you." Her words might sound perfectly innocent but the dark, hungry look in her eyes as she says them is anything but and it sets off my imagination once again.

How long is it until Amelia's bedtime?

I sit myself at the opposite end of the sofa to Leah in the hope her alluring scent might fade but it never does. It also means she's constantly in my line of vision every time I so much as glance at the TV. Not that I need to, I could recite Cinderella word for word with the amount of times I've been forced to sit through it over the years.

There are a million and one things I want to ask her, the most pressing is whether she's single or not, but Amelia ensures there's no time for adult conversation as she starts a debate with Leah about which Disney princess is the best and which one's hair they each would like. I've never wished for bedtime to come more in my life but having sat here with her almost in touching distance for the past hour is stretching my patience. I know that I probably shouldn't be alone with this woman but fuck if rational thinking isn't my priority right about now.

"CAN LEAH READ my bedtime story tonight?" Amelia asks when I eventually get through to her that it's bedtime. Even the tooth fairy visiting hasn't been enough of a pull to get her away from Leah. I'm strung too tightly right now to have an argument about her staying up later.

"Of course, but only if it's okay with her." I look to Leah, silently begging for her to agree and not to leave so I can do it myself.

"Um... sure. Although I've never read a bedtime story before. I might not be very good at it."

"It's like riding a bike, right, Dad?"

"Uh huh," I agree, just like I'm hoping sex will be after so long.

After kissing my little girl goodnight, I watch as they both leave the room. Amelia's still chatting away ten to the dozen.

Once they've rounded the corner, I stretch my tense body out and rest my head back against the sofa. What the hell am I playing at? She's too young and sweet for the likes of me. I should have let her leave earlier. I should have probably done a lot of things since I first saw her in the garden yesterday but I'm not totally onboard with following my own rules at this very moment.

Needing to keep busy in an attempt to get

thoughts of her out of my head, I take the dirty mugs through to the kitchen and place them in the dishwasher. The bag of veg she brought around catches my eye and inspiration strikes out of nowhere. Grabbing one of the many notebooks that litter my kitchen for such a moment, I start listing out ingredients for a potential new dish.

I lose myself in creating something new and it's not until a soft voice sounds out behind me that I realise I have company.

"She's exhausted; she fell asleep before I'd even finished."

Turning, I find Leah with her hip resting against the door frame with her eyes running over every inch of my body.

And fuck, my cock awakens yet again. It's not only the chilli causing temperatures to rise around here.

6

LEAH

STRANGE SHIT IS HAPPENING to me.

I'm twenty-one and it's almost the weekend. I should be making arrangements to get wasted. But no, here I am tucking a six-year-old into bed and reading her a bedtime story. I'm not stupid, I knew she'd try to get me to read the longest book she owns, but I spotted The Gruffalo and said I did great animal voices. She was asleep before I read the last page so I'm not sure if that was exhaustion or a reaction to my reading style. Truth is, I can't wait to get back downstairs to her daddy. There are gorgeous smells of tomato sauce and garlic coming from downstairs and I can hear pots and pans clattering around. The special ingredient in my hot chocolate seems to have gone straight to my head—I'm such a lightweight—and I'm feeling all sorts of confusing feelings.

This girl needs a mum.

I never thought about having kids before and now maybe I can see them in my future.

I don't really have much family now. Is that what's making me think of creating my own?

Jenson Hale is one sexy fucker.

———

WITH ONE LAST glance at how cute Amelia looks fast asleep, so angelic and peaceful, I close her bedroom door behind me softly and make my way downstairs.

"She's exhausted; she fell asleep before I'd even finished." I tell him as my eyes feast upon his body. The fitted fabric of his shorts makes his arse look delectable. The food aromas are making me hungry; Jenson's body is making me hungrier. I lick around my bottom lip as it feels a bit dry and Jenson groans.

"What's up?"

"Erm, cramp. A bit of cramp." He shakes out his foot.

"Do you want me to rub it for you?" I offer without thinking.

"Erm, no, it's okay." He flusters. "It's gone off now, just a twinge."

I move nearer to him and lean over the hob. "So what are you making? It smells divine."

"A new pasta sauce for the restaurant. I'm just experimenting at the moment for the autumn menu. The tomatoes and chilli in there are from your garden. I think your dad's chilli might just be my winning formula. He lifts up the spoon and holds it out to me to taste.

I open my mouth to accept the wooden spoon and the taste dances on my tongue. The burst of tomato, the underlying garlic and spices, and then that chilli kicker. "Wow." I exclaim. "That is superb."

"I've been experimenting for weeks with different ingredients and then you walk in tonight with that bag and bring me the magic. Amelia says I'm the magic one: magic fingers, magic hot chocolate. Looks like I have a rival for the role of magician.

I shrug. "It's my dad's magic really."

Jenson reaches over and touches my arm. I feel that electricity pass between us once more. "I'm sorry, Leah. It must be so difficult."

I nod. "Yeah, it is. I think I'll feel a little better

once the house is done and sold. It'll give me some closure."

But then I won't see you, I think.

"Are you hungry? I could fix some spaghetti to accompany this sauce and you can be my guinea pig and give me some feedback."

I bite my bottom lip while I wonder if I should admit to the fact I had a pizza delivered not all that long ago.

"Yeah, sure, just a small portion please."

He adds spaghetti to a pan and then picks up a bottle of red wine from the inbuilt wine rack. "I hardly ever drink being the sole carer for Amelia, but shall we live dangerously and open it?"

"Why not?" I reply. Given I've already shown him my arse I don't see how being a little tipsy might embarrass me any more than I was earlier. He pours a hefty slug into a glass for me, half a glass for himself and then adds a bit to his pasta sauce before tasting again.

"Almost there." He nods towards the circular small dining table. "Do you want to take a seat over there? I'll bring over some cutlery and the placemats."

Before long we're both seated and I have a plate of spaghetti in front of me. I tuck in and it's just everything. The most delicious meal I've ever tasted in my life, brought to the table by the most delicious man I've ever seen in my life. I feel a little nervous and keep drinking my wine. The next thing I know, Jenson has got up and is refilling my glass. "I really shouldn't. I'm not used to drinking."

He fills it up halfway, goes to the sink, grabbing a glass on his way and returns with a glass of water. "There you go. That should dilute the wine."

"I heard Amelia giggling this afternoon through the window, while I was painting." I blurt out. "I looked and she was being chased around by a woman. They looked to be having a ton of fun. Made me quite jealous to be indoors."

"Yes, Amelia loves her Auntie Kaylie. They're about the same age mentally."

I almost choke on a piece of spaghetti due to the fact I started laughing while I was chewing. "She's... what, your sister? Or your ex-wife's sister?"

"Mine, and seriously, I don't know what I would do without her. She looks after Amelia while I work, and she absolutely dotes on her. I do feel guilty though because I don't think she's fully living her own life, while she's busy in mine."

"Do you have no contact with your ex at all?"

"Oh, she sends Amelia birthday and Christmas

cards and some presents. Totally extravagant crap like designer handbags which she asks me to put away for when she's older. Apparently, they're an 'investment'. She could do with being a little more invested in our child. But no, she's too busy being a hotshot lawyer and having her photo taken for celebrity magazines while she rescues some poor sap who she only chose to help for their potential future headlines."

"Amicable divorce then?" I quip.

"She gave me custody of Amelia. I told her she could have anything else she wanted, but our daughter was mine. She didn't even fight for her." His jaw sets and I watch as he swallows, his Adam's apple bobbing up and down.

"I'm sorry." I think about the gorgeous little girl upstairs and I can't understand how anyone could leave her behind.

He looks up at me and smiles. "Don't be. We're so much happier without her. Christ knows what I saw in her in the first place."

I decide a change of conversation might be warranted, plus my head is starting to swim a little despite the food so I don't want to ask him about anything else that's personal.

"Tell me about your job."

At this he becomes visibly animated, telling me how he owns InHale after being a chef there, how it fits in with life as a single dad, but also means he can step into the kitchen when he likes. "You'll have to call in sometime and try me out," he says.

"Mmm, there's an offer I don't see I can refuse." My mouth has officially entered the 'speaking before thinking' zone.

For a moment, Jenson is stock still and then he growls, "Fuck it." The next thing I know he's dropped to his knees and his lips are on my own. I'm tasting Hot Daddy.

He breaks away from me, wiping his mouth.

"Fuck, Leah. I'm so sorry. I shouldn't have done that."

"Yes, you should." I half yell and then I pull his head towards mine.

I'm sitting on his dining chair, leaning down with a sex god at my feet. My hands run through his silken strands. He tastes of the dinner and red wine and he smells of masculinity. My hands trail down the side of his face running through the brush of his beard that tickles at my face. Our breathing is coming in short gasps as we feast on each other's mouths. Then we pull back.

"I'm too old for you, Leah? What are you, eighteen?"

"I'm twenty-one."

"You are?" He looks surprised. "But I'm ten years older than you. You should be with someone your own age."

This pisses me off and where I may have normally kept my mouth shut, the wine fires me up. "Way to go to make me feel like I'm about twelve years old." I push back on my chair away from him and stand. He stays on the floor looking up at me, regret in his gaze.

"I'm not a kid. I'm a fully-grown woman, and I knew exactly what was happening between us just now. Sexual attraction. It's been pulling between us all day, this chemistry, whether you want to admit it or not. It's a little ironic that I'm the one grown up enough to face the truth. When your balls drop, come find me. Until then, thanks for the dinner and the wine, but I'll be off now. I thought dessert might be on the cards but it seems it's way past my bedtime and my teddy bear is probably missing me."

"I- I'm..."

"Don't you dare tell me you're sorry again, or I will coat you in the remainder of the pasta sauce and hope the chilli burns your face off." I'm so sexually wound up and frustrated I want to have a full on slanging match but I'm not drunk enough to be unaware of Amelia being asleep upstairs so I just make sure there's plenty of venom in my tone.

I pick up my shoulder bag and head for the door. "I'd say fuck you, but seeing as that's kind of the issue here, I'll just tell you to go. Screw. Yourself."

With that I flick my hair and turn to the door where I stomp out all the way back to my own home. Then I throw myself on my bed and cry tears of frustration for the shit storm my life is right now.

7

JENSON

"FUUUUCK!" I roar once the sound of the slammed front door resonates through the entire house.

The entire time I sat with her at the table and watched her lap up my spaghetti, all I could think about were her lips. Her full, red, soft lips. I needed them on me more than I needed my next breath and the state of my blue balls after a day of having her front and centre of all my thoughts meant I allowed my cock to take the lead and I acted like an arsehole.

It had been so long since I felt a woman beneath my fingers that the pull to her was too much. I dropped to my knees in front of her, practically begging her to return my kiss like the desperate fucker that I am.

Her lips were everything I'd been imagining all

day. The second their warmth pressed against mine, I lost all control. My tongue impatiently pushed inside so I could taste her. I explored every inch of her mouth, her movement matching my own as her hands started to wander, but it was all too soon that I allowed reality back in and pulled back from her.

Kissing her was wrong, even her being here on a Thursday night was wrong. Much like my sister, she should be out with friends, spending time trying to find a nice guy her own age to spend time with, not the lonely and pathetic guy next door.

Grabbing the plates from the table I throw them into the sink. Their crash and shatter as they hit the ceramic settles something inside of me, but it only lasts a few seconds before I need more. Swiping my notebook and some of the utensils I'd left littering the counter, I watch them all hit the floor to a chorus clattering.

Scrubbing my hand down my face, I place my other against the counter and hang my head in shame. It's only made worse when I hear something behind me.

"Is everything okay, Daddy?"

"Fuck," I whisper, trying to school my features before I turn around and face my daughter.

"Of course, sweetheart. Everything's fine. Go on back to bed."

"But I heard a loud crash. Where's Leah?" she asks, looking around with her brows pulled together in concern.

"She had to go home." Disappointment tugs at my stomach knowing she had to leave because of me.

"Oh." The sadness that covers her little face guts me. It might have only been a day, but it seems it's not just me that's a little taken with our new neighbour.

"Come on, let's go and tuck you back in."

It only takes minutes for her to doze off again, leaving me alone with my fucked-up thoughts once more.

When I need to escape my reality, my fucked-up world, I cook. So once I'm confident that Amelia is asleep again, I shut the kitchen door, power up my wireless speaker and set to work. Those vegetables Leah brought around have inspired me and there's no time like the present.

I FEEL like a fucking zombie the next morning when a happy and smiling Amelia comes bounding into my room. I eventually crashed sometime after four am once the fridge and almost all the counter in the kitchen was covered in freshly made dishes and sauces.

"Isn't it a bit early?" I groan when she hops up into bed with me.

My body immediately tenses knowing that I've woken with a raging hard on after my dream about the kiss between Leah and I continuing further than the kitchen table.

"It's almost seven, Daddy. Aunt Kaylie will be here soon and you'll be late for work."

Christ, what has my life become? I've got a six-year-old chastising me for going to bed late.

"Why don't you go and put the TV on? I'll be down to make breakfast in a few minutes." The throbbing of my cock tells me that I'm in no state to follow her right now.

She hops off the bed and runs towards the door, giving me hope for a few minutes of peace to do what I need to do but at the last minute she turns her smiling face to me.

"Pancakes?"

"I said it was beans on toast this morning." I try

to keep my voice strong, but I have a hard time fighting her when she looks at me like that.

"But pancakes are my favourite."

"I know, baby. Go and put that TV on and we'll see."

The sound of her little feet hitting the stairs fills my ears. I hear the sound of the TV and then lower my hand and set about relieving myself of the tension that is burning hot through me.

"PLEASE, don't tell me you made her pancakes again?" my sister groans when she appears and finds my frying pan still hot on the hob. I really didn't have it in me to argue with a child this morning so I took the easiest option. "Are you okay, you look exhausted?" She changes tack when I turn and she gets a look at my tired face.

"Yeah, I was just up late working."

"Are you sure you can afford to have this weekend off?"

"Of course. Nothing is going to stop me giving you some time to yourself."

She looks conflicted. I know she wants to have a life of her own but being here with us and her pretending to be a mum to Amelia is much easier for her.

"Okay," she concedes. "Any instructions for today?"

"Nope, just the usual. Not too much TV and no shit food."

Her eyebrow raises as she looks past me to the half-eaten pancake sitting on a plate. "Riiight."

Grabbing a load of stuff from the counter, we repeat yesterday's routine as she holds the front door open for me followed by the boot of my car. But unlike yesterday, Leah doesn't appear. In fact, I see no movement at all from inside her house. Something inside me aches knowing that I hurt her last night. Kaylie looks between me and Leah's house suspiciously, but she doesn't ask.

"Thank you. I promise I won't be late."

"No rush." She waves me off and rushes back inside when Amelia shouts.

Glancing back at Leah's, I grab one of the tubs and quickly jog up her path to place it on her doorstep. It might not be much, but I feel better knowing I've made the first move to apologise for last night, even if I took the pussy way out and dropped it and ran.

"MORNING, BOSS MAN." Scott, one of my waiters, sings when I step through the door. He's busy setting up service ready for the doors to open for breakfast in a few short minutes. "Looks like you might have got lucky last night. Anyone you need to introduce me to?"

The thought of allowing Leah to meet notorious ladies man Scott sends a shiver racing down my spine. I can't deny that she'd probably be better off with him though. They're a similar age without any ties that come with kids. Knowing both of them, I actually think they'd probably hit it off which is even more reason not to mention her right now. I might be all kinds of wrong for my hot next-door neighbour but I'm a selfish arsehole and I want her for myself.

"Nah, just working."

"And you didn't do enough of that all day here yesterday? You need to let your hair down, Boss. All work, no play—"

"Yeah, yeah," I cut him off knowing exactly where he's going. "You about ready? We've got quite a few breakfast reservations this morning?"

"Ready and waiting." Scott salutes me and I

chuckle at his ridiculousness as I make my way to the kitchen and then my office.

It's late afternoon when I finally give up and head for home. My body aches and my eyes sting with my need for sleep, plus I need to let Kaylie go so she can get started on her weekend.

"Daddy," Amelia squeals when she hears me come through the front door. "You're early." The smile on her face melts my heart and reminds me of another reason I told my sister I'd sort out the weekend off. I've been working too hard and need some quality time with my girl.

"I thought maybe we could go swimming?"

"Yessss," she squeals and immediately turns and runs up the stairs to get ready.

"You're free," I say, walking into the kitchen to find my sister handwashing the dishes I've left littering the counters last night. "We've got a dishwasher you know?"

"I know. I just prefer doing it by hand."

"Whatever you say. So what are the plans for the weekend?"

"I've no idea. I just said yes to a couple of offers from my colleagues at work to go out." She winces with uncertainty.

"Just try to enjoy yourself, Kay."

"I'll do my best." She turns and dries her hands on a towel before collecting her bag from the sideboard in the hall. "Just promise you'll call me if you need me."

"Sure," I lie. I've no intention of ruining her weekend.

SHUTTING everything else in my life down, I focus on my little girl and the quality time we so desperately need.

We end up in the swimming pool long after our allotted time and when we eventually emerge our skin is covered in wrinkles but seeing the smile on Amelia's face makes it all worth it.

We stop off at a pub on the way home and fill our empty bellies with burgers and ice cream. By the time we're pulling onto our driveway later that night Amelia can hardly keep her eyes open.

"Straight up to bed for you," I say, turning the engine off and looking in the rear-view mirror. Her response is a yawn, telling me she agrees.

She slowly climbs out and drags her tired legs towards the front door. I tell myself not to do it, but right at the last minute my eyes flick over to Leah's house. My stomach lurches in excitement when I spot some movement in one of the bedroom windows. Was she watching us?

Shaking the crazy thoughts from my head, I push the key into our lock and we both step inside. I screwed up last night. She hates me and rightly so after I made her out to be nothing more than a child when I know in reality that she's so much more than that. If her body isn't evidence enough, then the way she kissed with such confidence and passion surely was.

My cock stirs once again as I think back to our short but incredible kiss. My muscles ache for me to go over there and apologise properly but Amelia needs to be my priority. I'm too good a dad, or at least I hope I am, to put her to bed and immediately run next door to have some fun of my own.

Knowing I've got the weekend off means I allow myself to just chill out on the sofa watching some kind of war film on the TV. I don't pay all that much attention to it but being able to forget about the restaurant for just a few hours is a huge relief. So much so that the next thing I know, it's gone midnight and I'm having to drag my sleep-heavy body from the sofa and up to bed.

8

LEAH

WHEN I WAKE on Friday morning, I feel a wave of embarrassment hit for the way I behaved. Yes, he pissed me off, but too much alcohol had made me basically have a grown-up tantrum. He was right. I was young. A lot younger than him. But try telling my body that, which craves him on waking.

Hearing a car, I jump out of bed and stand at the front bedroom window out of sight. I see him dash up my path. As he does so he's looking for me, his eyes searching the house, but I remain in the shadows. I told him to find his balls but instead he's left something on the path. I'm so fucking frustrated in more ways than one.

After getting dressed, I head downstairs, open

the door, and find a tub on the path with a note on top stuck on with some sticky tape.

Sorry! Here's a peace offering! J.

Lifting the lid on the tub, his spicy sauce's aroma dances up my nostrils and my stomach rumbles. *I bet Amelia had pancakes this morning.* The thought comes out of left field. I've only known them a couple of days and they're taking over my brain. I need to focus on myself and the things I need to get done.

I spend the day decorating and making Carl cups of tea. Occasionally, I spy out of the back window to see if Amelia's out there. I don't feel as obsessed with looking now I know the woman is Jenson's sister. I'm becoming pathetic. It's time to look over my project plans for the house and step it all up a gear so that I can be out of here as soon as possible. I need a fresh start, someplace new.

The last few years I'd been at Uni, living in a shared house with other students while I passed my Early Years degree. I was all lined up to start a new job when the call that changed my life forever came. And I learned just who my friends were by the fact that not a single one of them has called to ask how I am. But in some ways that's perfect. I can move anywhere, work anywhere, live anywhere.

I'm not without family. I have aunties, uncles, cousins. We're just not all that close and I'm not comfortable with changing that right now. I know they're worried about me, having lost my mum and dad, but trying to forge a relationship with me now just seems too little too late.

God, I'm miserable today. Even Carl notices it.

"Oi, short stack. What are you doing tonight?" He asks as I wander in with another cup of tea for him.

"Having a wild night in, decorating."

"No, you're not. I'll pick you up at eight. We're going out on the town."

I shake my head but he puts a hand up. "I'm not asking you on a date. There are a few of us go out every Friday night, guys and girls. You need to go out. I'm not prying but I overhear stuff on phone calls, and rumours fly around this area. I know you've suffered a great loss, Leah, but it's time for you to put the paintbrush down and paint the town instead. His hands are folded across his chest.

"You're not going to take no for an answer, are you?"

"Nope."

"So where is it we're going?"

Soho. I'll come call for you at eight and we'll catch the Tube there together, otherwise I know you'll bottle it and be a no show.

He's not wrong. I'd put my pyjamas on and go to bed.

SO THAT'S how I find myself drinking in the Brewdog bar on a Friday night. This evening I'm dressed in my own style of black skinny fit capri pants and a red v-neck tight blouse that shows off my cleavage to its best advantage. It's chilli red and I wonder if somehow my subconscious knew that when I picked it out of the wardrobe earlier.

The bar is a vast space with concrete walls and floors and chain-link across the ceilings. Pendant lights hang from red cord and the furniture is sparse and simple. Not that you can spot much of it on this packed Friday night. "How the hell are we going to get served in here?" I yell at Carl. I'll have no voice soon above this racket.

"Helps if you know the bar staff," he says and nods indicating that I should follow him to the bar. He pushes his way to one end and putting his fingers in his mouth lets out an ear-piercing whistle. I watch as a small black-haired woman with smoky black eyes and a bright red lips turns towards him, revealing a nose piercing. She sticks her middle finger up at him and carries on serving.

"That went well." I yell again.

"She'll be here in a minute." Carl says. "She's my cousin."

"Ah. Handy to have relatives in a busy bar on a Friday night." I shout.

He nods and answers, "Suki," showing he clearly didn't hear a word I said. I guess that's the name of the little spitfire behind the bar. She heads over after serving and gives Carl a chin tilt.

"Hey, cous. Usual?"

"Yeah, please, and..." He looks at me and Suki follows suit.

"Jack and coke please." I ask.

Suki raises an eyebrow. "Well, shit, thought you'd ask for a coke and a straw given you look about fifteen. Thought about ID-ing you."

I raise my own middle finger at her and she howls with laughing.

"I like this one," she says to Carl.

"Not a date." He shouts. "She's currently my boss."

Suki goes off to get the drinks.

"My cousin acts all spunky and to a large extent she is, but she does have a soft side; or she did when she was younger anyway. I only see her now when we're out."

"Huh, I don't see mine at all." I shout again.

He looks at me with an expression of sadness and pity and I don't need it. I'm out in London on a Friday night. I've made the effort. I'm dressed up and drinking and I'm going to damn well enjoy myself. It's time to make some new friends and start as I mean to go on. I pull at his shirt sleeve once we have our drinks. "Come on, let's get back to the others."

It's a great night. The alcohol loosens the restraints I've put around myself and I'm pleased that Carl doesn't try to hit on me. A couple of the guys there talk to me and show interest, mainly in my tits, but it's nice. And I chat, well, shout, to a few of the girls too. They tell me I'm more than welcome to come again.

I arrive back at my own house alone, merry, and it's a completely different feeling from the night before's tears. My tummy rumbles and although it's half past midnight, I warm up the sauce Jenson left for me. Drunken me can't be bothered to cook pasta so I dip bread and crisps in it. It's still delicious. I collapse into bed and dream of kisses at dining tables.

THE NEXT MORNING, I wake in desperate need of coffee and to a banging noise at my front door.

What the actual fuck?

I walk from my bedroom to the room at the front and look out of the window to find Jenson at the door. What does he want? I open the window and shout down to him.

"Yeah?"

He looks up and I see his eyes widen before I realise that from this position my boobs are threatening to leave my pyjama shirt. Well, I've flashed him my arse, and now almost my rack. Why don't I just walk naked across his lawn? Actually, I sigh, I'd like to do that across his bedroom.

"Erm, sorry to disturb you, but I've been called into work on an emergency and I gave my sister the weekend off so I've no one for Amelia. I just wondered if you could stay with her, just for an hour? I can take her with me but it's not an ideal place to be amongst chefs who use the f-word as often as they use the word 'the'.

ANGEL DEVLIN & TRACY LORRAINE

"Sure, give me ten to get dressed. Be making me some coffee." I shout and then I shut the window.

I check out the state of me in the mirror. Mascara streaked eyes and bedhead. Great. Good job his eyes were mainly on my breasts. Men. Says I'm too young for him but it doesn't stop him checking me out, does it? Anyway, this is about looking after Amelia. So whatever mixed emotions I have right now about her father, I'll do this for her.

I grab the fastest shower in history, braid my wet hair into a plait, and then I deliberately seek out a short skirt, tights, and a t-shirt. I look like a naughty schoolgirl. Slipping my feet into my trainers I head next door.

"I'm here." I say as I push through the left ajar door.

"Leah, I'm in the kitchen." Amelia yells. "I'm having pancakes. Do you want one?"

"I haven't got time, Amelia." I hear Jenson say as I reach the kitchen. His mouth drops open when he sees me. Good, that's just the reaction I wanted.

"Morning, Amelia." I say brightly. "I can try to cook pancakes."

"Cool," she says following it up with her gappy-toothed grin. "So when did you lose the tooth?" I ask.

"Thursday morning. My auntie says it's all the

sugary stuff on my pancakes making my teeth fall out but it's happening to Rory at school and his family are sugar free vegans so she's talking crap."

"Amelia!"

Amelia giggles.

"So," I turn to Jenson. "I brought around my certificates to show you that I actually have a degree in childcare, so you can rest easy knowing your child is in the hands of an expert."

He nods but doesn't ask to see them.

"Look at them." I shake them at him.

"Fine." He gives them a cursory glance and hands them back to me.

"Right, well, got to get to work." He lifts his jacket from the back of the dining chair. "Like I say, I should only be an hour or so."

I shrug him off. "Take your time. I'm having a day off from decorating."

"Sick of the smell of paint?"

"That and I woke with a bit of a sore head. I went out last night drinking in Soho with Carl and—"

His eyes narrow. "Oh, you're not still under the influence, are you?"

"Yes, I'm drunk and in charge of your child. Do

you have any more alcohol in the cupboards I can add to my coffee?" I say sarcastically.

"Sorry, that was a stupid thing to say. Thank you for looking after Amelia. It means a lot. I'll repay the favour by helping you in the garden tomorrow. I can see it needs someone a little taller to deal with some of the larger shrubs."

"Daddy said he liked your bush." Amelia says.

My eyes widen.

"The Magnolia. It's thriving in your garden." Jenson explains.

A smirk dances around my lips and I watch as his own curls at my reaction.

"Kids." He mutters under his breath and then with a kiss and a hug with his daughter, he tells us he'll see us later and then it's just me, Amelia, batter and a pan. What could possibly go wrong?

"YOU REALLY CAN'T DO PANCAKES." Amelia voices the obvious.

The first one got stuck to the pan.

The second one was far too thick and disgusting.

The third (and last of the batter) was glorious

until I tried to throw it, where half stuck to the ceiling and the other half fell to the floor.

"Yup. Think we'd better leave pancake making to your daddy." I said. "But I tell you what I'm really good at."

"Yeah?"

"Playing princesses, so let's go grab our tiaras."

9

JENSON

I RUSH through the entrance to the restaurant, my haste turning every head in my direction including the lady I should have been here to greet thirty minutes ago. How the hell I managed to miss an email about her visit, God only knows.

"Morning, Boss. Would you like a coffee?"

"Yes. Yes, please." What I really need is a strong whiskey but seeing as it's barely past nine am I don't think it would be a good idea.

Sucking in a large breath, I turn towards the woman who pretty much holds the key to my future. If this goes well then it could seal the restaurant's reputation for years to come. Go badly and... I shudder. I can't even comprehend it.

"Hi, I'm so sorry I'm late. Jenson, Jenson Hale."

"It's no problem. Scott was telling me all about your little girl." She glances up at him and I swear her cheeks redden.

Looking over my shoulder, I follow her stare, my eyes begging Scott not to screw this up for me, despite screwing things being his main pastime.

"Anyway," she says regaining my focus. "I'm Kelly Sotherland, and I'm a restaurant reviewer from The Sunday Times." My heart skips a beat just hearing the words. This is it; this is the moment that could change my life. "I have to say Mr. Hale that I'm very impressed with InHale. I've actually dined here on two occasions and each time the food, service, and ambiance have been exquisite."

My lips twitch up into a smile and I'm reminded all over again why I became a chef in the first place. I wanted to show people what good food was. It certainly wasn't the meals I was brought up on. I love my mother dearly, but she can't cook for shit. I could only ever dream of owning my own restaurant as a kid. I've had to work incredibly hard to be where I am today and to be sitting here with a well-respected reviewer telling me how much she loves it here, well it's everything.

"Thank you so much, you've no idea how much that means to me."

"No, no. Thank you."

She goes quiet as Scott comes over with coffees. Her face heats once again making me want to groan in frustration. Scott's eyes don't leave her as she orders her breakfast. I know it's not very politically correct of me, but his looks are one of the reasons I hired him. I just knew those along with his charisma and sense of humour he would be a total hit with our customers. And it seems I was right because right now he has our toughest customer eating out of the palm of his hands.

I'M BUZZING by the time I shake Kelly's hand and show her to the exit. Taking a seat at the bar, I wait for Scott to come over.

"Where's Krissy?" I ask referring to our missing bartender.

"No idea, she was meant to be here almost an hour ago."

"Fucking hell," I mutter, pulling my phone from my pocket and scrolling through to find her number.

Voicemail. Fantastic.

"What are we going to do, we've got a full lunch service booked in?"

"Looks like I'm pulling pints this afternoon." It's not exactly what I wanted to do after the high of this morning's interview, but I don't have a lot of choice seeing as customers are already loitering outside ready to fill the place.

"You know how to do that, Boss?"

"Ha, funny. I started in this industry at the very bottom. I've waited and pulled pints with the best of 'em."

"Fair enough. Zoey's due in at six but might be worth a call to see if she can get in early."

"Thanks for that." I don't mean to snap but I also don't need Scott telling me how to run my business.

"Boss." He salutes before heading out across the restaurant to begin taking orders.

Thankfully, a quick call to Zoey results in her agreeing to come in a little early. I feel awful for doing it, but I know I can't leave Amelia with Leah any longer. She's got more important things to be doing than bailing me out. I'm surprised she even agreed after what happened the last time we were together. I guess my peace offering must have gone down well.

I'm just about ready to crash after the adrenaline from this morning's interview and then a shift behind the bar, but as I pull up on to my driveway a new lease of excitement races through me.

Picturing how she looked when I left this morning in that shirt and tiny bloody skirt, my mouth waters and my fists clench with my need to get my hands on her.

Blowing out a breath to calm my thoughts, I remind myself that I'm also about to walk in to see Amelia.

"Hello?" I shout into the house when all I'm greeted with is silence. My heart begins to race that something's happened and I wasn't informed. My imagination starts to run wild when the sound of joyful laughter from the garden fills my ears. I immediately relax and feel ridiculous for jumping to conclusions. I know Amelia's in safe hands, but as a parent I think it's natural to assume the worst.

Walking through the kitchen, I place down the food I brought home for dinner before making my way out. I'm just about to step down onto the patio when the sight in front of me has my body freezing up.

Leah and Amelia are in the middle of a water fight. They've got a super soaker each as they laugh, squeal, and chase each other around. Once I know Amelia is okay, I turn my focus on Leah. Her white shirt is soaked and totally see through; her skirt is sodden and stuck to her thighs revealing her now shapely tight-less legs. Lifting my gaze, I find her hair dripping, sticking to the sides of her face and down her neck. Her make-up is smeared all down her cheeks and her eyes shine in delight. She's never looked more beautiful.

Holy shit.

My jeans suddenly feel too small for my body as my cock swells behind the confining fabric.

I watch them for the longest time with my heart threatening to pound out of my chest. There is something so right about the image before me and I'm also a little too happy about it continuing.

"Hey, Daddy's home," Amelia squeals, running over and blasting me in the chest with ice cold water.

"Oh you are in so much trouble." I take off after her and she runs as fast as her legs will carry her.

She giggles and screams the closer I get, but I soon learn that I'm not only fighting against a six-year-old but also a slightly older and sexier woman when another stream of water hits my back.

My arm wraps around Amelia's waist when I catch up to her. She kicks and screams as I head for the pool I've set up at the end of the garden.

"Daddy, no. Daddy, don't dunk... DADDY!" She squeals as I throw her into the freezing water. She soon finds her footing but not before Leah rushes over still wielding her super soaker.

The next thirty minutes I think are the most joyful of my life as the three of us run around the garden acting like kids, getting totally soaked and loving every minute of it.

"Okay, okay. I think I'm done." I say between my heaving breaths as I bend over with my hands on my knees. "I'm too old for this."

"No chance, you're in better shape than me by a mile and I'm still going." Leah laughs, her eyes dropping down to where my t-shirt is clinging to every indent and muscle of my chest and stomach.

"Is that right?" Reaching behind me, I pull the fabric from my body. I want to say it's seamless, but it sticks more than I was expecting and takes a good bit of force to get it over my head.

Exactly as I intended, her eyes drop once again to feast on my exposed skin. Her teeth sink into her bottom lip and it's the perfect distraction I need. She doesn't even notice when I step towards her, but she soon realises when I lift her from the ground, throw her over my shoulder and begin marching back to the pool.

"Jenson, don't you dare. Jenson, Jenson, nooooo."

Stepping into the pool, I plunge her under the water, cutting off her screams.

Releasing her, I allow her to find her feet, but I soon realise my mistake as she flies at me. Taking me by surprise, I just about grab her before my feet slide out from under me and together we fall back into the water.

Her laughter warms my heart, but her face soon stills when she looks down and finds me staring at her.

My fingers tighten around her waist and I pull her body so it's flush against mine. There's no denying what her being this close and soaking wet does to me and when her lips part in surprise I know she feels it.

"Jenson, I—"

"Come on, you two," Amelia shouts, oblivious to the moment happening between us.

"We should get out. I'm soaked."

"Is that right?" Her eyes widen and her cheeks heat. It's enough to know that she's very much wet and ready for me right now.

"Shit."

She scrambles off me and climbs from the pool. I

give it a few seconds in the hope my cock realises she's no longer touching it before following.

"I should go," Leah says, glancing over towards her house.

"No, please don't go," Amelia begs, plastering a sad expression on her face that I know is going to pull at Leah's heartstrings. "You promised we could watch Aladdin."

"I said if your dad wasn't home then we could watch it. He's here now and I'm sure he's got plans for the two of you."

My heart lurches at the thought of her leaving already. "Yeah, I have got plans actually." Leah's face drops ever so slightly but it's enough to make my stomach clench with anticipation for what the rest of this night might hold. "I was hoping you'd join us for dinner."

"Me?" she asks, as if I could possibly mean anyone else.

"Yes, you. I brought stuff home from the restaurant. It just needs warming up. Let's go and get dry and I'll dish it up."

"Okay. If you're sure?"

"I'm pretty sure I've not been surer of anything in my life," I whisper in her ear when I get to her and I delight in the shudder that runs through her body.

Amelia runs inside to shower while Leah and I tidy up the garden.

"How long will dinner be? I'll just go back next door and—" Thoughts of her leaving have me panicking.

"Minutes. Just shower here, I'll find you something clean to put on." The image of her in one of my shirts is suddenly the only thing I can think about and I know I need to do anything to ensure it happens. "Come on, I'll show you to my en-suite. You can get cleaned up and then I'll have dinner ready."

I don't give her a chance to argue. I take her hand in mine and all but drag her up the stairs.

"The towels are clean and the shower's incredible. I'll put something for you to wear on the bed. Come and join us when you're ready."

Regretfully, I pull the door closed, leaving her standing in the middle of my en-suite like a lost sheep. My body aches to walk back inside and join her in the shower. If I didn't have Amelia to take care of, I'd probably throw caution to the wind and do just that. But instead, I rummage through my wardrobe for a shirt and pull a brand-new pair of boxers from inside my drawer. I drop the box beside them on the bed so she knows I'm not leaving a dirty old pair for her to wear and I leave the room, pulling the door closed behind me with some dry clothes for myself in hand.

After checking on Amelia and finding her some clean pyjamas, I have the quickest shower of my life in the main bathroom before pulling on a pair of shorts and heading down to sort out dinner. I know I should put a shirt on but I tell myself that it's a humid evening and I would be too hot. In reality I know it's because I love the way she bites on her bottom lip and the colour her cheeks go every time she checks me out.

10

LEAH

DO NOT PANIC.

Do not panic.

Do NOT...

My breath comes in short gasps... GAH.

I'm under the shower jets and wondering what's on the agenda for when I head back downstairs.

I try to tell myself it's just a thank you for my childcare.

But my mind and body know it's not. I felt his rock-hard dick pushing against me as I pressed up against him in the water.

He wants me.

I want him.

My instinct is to leap out of the shower and get back downstairs as quickly as I can, but I make myself play it cool and take my time. I'm faced with the choice of Amelia's strawberry shower gel or Jenson's manly spice one and I choose his. I want to smell like him, a prelude to the main event. I do not want to smell like a six-year-old and put him off touching me. Because I need him to touch me so damn badly I can barely stand.

Wrapping myself in a towel, I exit the shower and make my way into Jenson's bedroom. It's all warm browns and walnut wood and it smells of his aftershave. I have to stop myself from picking up his pillow and sniffing it. Spotting the pale-blue shirt and white boxers, I put them on. The shirt is a soft cotton and the aroma of his wash powder pervades the air around me. I towel dry my hair and leave it, hoping it looks beachy. If Amelia wasn't downstairs, I'd have gone down in the towel and dropped it at his feet.

"Leah! You forgot your skirt or trousers, silly." Amelia giggles from her place at the table where she's eating some kind of casserole. There's a smell of beef and wine and sure enough on closer inspection it's beef bourguignon.

"Leah's waiting for her clothes to dry, baby girl."

"Daddy, how many more times. I am not a baby."

I watch as Jenson leans over and kisses Amelia

on the forehead. "And how many times have I told you that you'll always be my baby."

"Even when I'm a hundred?"

"Even when you're a hundred, *baby girl*."

I don't realise that I have the most stupid look on my face from watching this sweet exchange until Jenson looks back at me and then dips his head as if he feels a little conspicuous and on show.

"Take a seat and I'll bring yours over. Do you want wine?"

I shake my head. "Just water please." If anything happens between us tonight, I want to be perfectly sober so I can remember every last detail.

I hitch myself onto the chair and feeling eyes on me, I turn to see Jenson's gaze running up my thighs all the way to my chest where the tops of my breasts are just visible through the top of the shirt where I've left it unbuttoned.

"My shirt looks good on you," he says, his voice lower and gruffer.

There's a tension in the room, like we're being held back in the stretch of an elastic band, where at any moment it's going to snap.

"Have you nearly finished your dinner, Amelia, because you need to be in bed soon? It's getting late."

Amelia smacks her lips together. "That is yummy, Daddy. More please."

I want to laugh as I witness the frustration in Jenson's expression as he takes her plate and adds a few more spoonfuls of food. "Not too much more as I don't want your belly too full or you'll not sleep."

"Daddy, it's Friday and Leah is here. We're watching Aladdin."

"It's late, that will have to be another day."

A spoon drops hard against a plate. "No. We already agreed it, didn't we, Leah? Aladdin, and we are going to pretend my teapot is the lamp and we're sitting on the rug to watch it because that's our magic carpet." I can recognise that Amelia is overtired and on the edge of a full blown meltdown.

"Let's finish our food very quickly and put the film on, shall we?" I say, turning to Jenson and winking. He shrugs his shoulders, clearly not understanding my plan.

Food finished, I follow Amelia into the living room where I pull the rug in front of the sofa so our backs can lean against it, and we press play on the film while I put a cosy throw around mine and Amelia's shoulders.

Not six minutes into the film, she's fallen fast asleep. Jenson walks into the room having tidied up the kitchen and he freezes in place while he watches Amelia fast asleep in my arms. There's a wistfulness to his gaze and I know it's connected with the fact that Amelia's mother isn't here doing what I'm doing. His facial expressions couldn't be clearer if his thoughts appeared in balloons beside his mouth.

"Give her another few minutes to get into a deeper sleep and then you can take her upstairs." I tell him. I don't know what I expect him to do but it's not to curl up at the other side of Amelia so that she's sandwiched between us.

It's far too intimate for how long we've known each other and yet it feels so *right*. I want this man and I adore his cute as a button daughter. This wasn't in my plan. We don't even talk as we sit there, Aladdin paused. Dusk is settling on the evening and a cool breeze enters from the open window, hitting my arms as I unfurl myself from the throw.

"You'd better take her upstairs." I say.

He nods.

"I ought to go."

He shakes his head.

"No. Stay. Right here. Right on this rug. Stay. I'll be back as soon as I can."

I watch as he carries his daughter out of the room as if she's the weight of a packet of popcorn rather than a lanky-legged six-year-old. His shorts hug his arse and I don't take my eyes off it until he's gone.

Then I sit still, wrapping the blanket back tight around myself while my heart beats faster in anticipation of what's to come.

Hopefully, me.

His footsteps come back down the stairs and I'm frozen in place on the rug with the throw wrapped around me.

His eyes meet mine.

"You'll not be needing that to keep you warm." His voice is thick with lust.

"Come take it off." I invite.

He stalks in my direction and I can see the shape of his cock through his shorts, straining the zipper. I swallow, my mouth going dry while somewhere else gets wet.

He kneels in front of me on the rug and slips the throw off my shoulders. It feels like he's stripped me bare.

"God, I've thought of nothing but this all the damn day."

"Me too." I admit.

His mouth meets mine, gently at first, soft brushes of his lips against my own and then he presses firmer. I open my mouth and his tongue slips inside tangling with my own.

We're an inferno, as the fire between us rages out of control.

"As much as my shirt looks fucking awesome on you, I need it off." He growls, unbuttoning it until it reveals my breasts.

"Christ." He groans, slipping the shirt off my shoulders.

He pushes me back onto the rug and takes a cushion from the sofa placing it under my head. Then he's done with my comfort levels as his mouth drops to take a nipple within. I can feel his beard tickling my skin as he moves. He sucks hard and nips gently and I thrust my chest up towards him wanting more, needing more. He moves to the other nipple but as much as I'm enjoying it, I don't want him there, I *need* him elsewhere.

"Jenson, please."

He releases my nipple and chuckles. It's a beautiful sound. Then his eyes meet mine and he raises a brow.

"Please what?"

I feel myself blush.

"Please fuck me, Jenson."

"All in good time." He winks and then he moves further down to the apex of my thighs.

He grabs hold of his boxers and pulls them off me, discarding them somewhere on the floor.

Spreading my thighs further apart I feel his breath at my core and then his tongue flicks across my clit and I arch towards his mouth.

"Oh fuck."

"You taste better than any dish I've ever served." He utters before his mouth descends once more. He enters me with his tongue, dipping in and out and then licking back up my seam until I can barely remember my own name. But I can remember his.

"Jenson, Oh shit, yes. Jenson."

And then I explode over his tongue. He holds me, his hands firmly under my arse as I rock against him until I come down from my high.

My breathing is fast as he comes back up, so we're eye to eye. "Now I'm going to fuck you," he says.

"Yeah, you might need to take off your shorts first."

"Such impatience. You desperate for my cock, you dirty girl?"

I want to scream yes, because his words are making my core slicker. I reach for his waistband and he helps me open the fastening and lower the zipper. It's a struggle because of the size of his rock-hard cock. I sit up and lower his shorts down and then Jenson groans with impatience, stands up and kicks them off and his boxers follow quickly. And then I'm licking around my lips and grabbing his hand and pulling him back towards me on the rug until he's once again nestled between my thighs, having put on a condom on which was conveniently in his pocket.

Then he's in me, pushing all the way to the hilt and I groan, wrapping my legs around him to bring him as deep as I can. We find our rhythm quickly, Jenson almost pulling all the way out teasing me and then slamming back in. He circles my bud with his fingertip while thrusting inside me and I feel myself begin to climb once more.

"Jenson, I'm going to..."

He thrusts harder and faster and a fine sheen of sweat forms on his forehead. He stiffens and then he releases one last hard thrust and takes me over with him. We cling together as we ride out the waves of pleasure.

"That was... fuck... that was amazing, Leah. Thank you."

I giggle and it breaks any awkwardness between us.

"Did you just thank me for the fuck?"

Jenson covers his face with his hands. "I'm not very good at talking to women."

"Well, thank you, Jenson, for the fuck. It was awesome."

We both start laughing. He grabs the blanket, wraps it around our naked bodies and we stay like that for a long while.

———

EVENTUALLY, I begin to get cold and the rug is not so comfortable.

"It's late. I'd better make a move."

"You can stay?"

"No, it would be awkward in the morning with Amelia. And it's not like I have far to go home is it?"

"Well let me go see if your own clothes are dry now and then I'll walk you home."

And he does. He walks me all the way to my door where he pushes me against it, claiming my mouth once more. Finally, after a couple of minutes, he breaks the kiss. "And now I have a raging hard on again."

I put my hand down between us and stroke him through his shorts.

"Not helping."

I giggle and drop my hand, going in my bag for my keys.

"Thank you for a lovely evening. I'll see you, er—"

"Tomorrow. You will see us tomorrow. Come for breakfast."

I don't hesitate to reply.

"Okay. But only if it's pancakes."

"Deal. I'll teach you how to cook them without getting the mixture all over the ceiling and floor."

I shove him in the arm. "Go on, show off. Back to your own house."

He laughs and I watch him walk back to his own front door. He shakes his arse at me before he goes inside.

It's going to be a long time until the morning.

11

JENSON

WALKING AWAY from Leah last night after taking her home felt wrong. My body was desperate to be pressed up against her once again. Hell, my cock was already trying to break through my shorts to get to her, but I knew it was the right thing to do. I'm not a young, free, and single guy anymore. I've got responsibilities and I can no longer follow what my cock wants. Now I've got to think of the most important thing in my life, my daughter. The last thing I need is her thinking that Leah is some kind of permanent fixture in her life when in reality I've no clue if that's going to be the case. I fucking want it to be but it's not just my decision to make and I'm fully aware she's not just signing up to be with me. The facts are, I come with a ready-made family and she's only twenty-one.

I drive myself crazy as I lie in bed going through all the possibilities when it comes to a serious relationship with Leah. I know it's what I want but she'd have every right to run as fast as she could right about now.

When I do eventually fall asleep, it's fitful at best. It's full of dreams about her curves, her taste, her soft moans of pleasure as she was about to fall over the edge and her sexy demands for more.

I shouldn't be surprised that when I wake, my cock is already tenting the duvet. Thankfully, I'm up before Amelia stirs so it gives me a chance to give the house a once over. Leah may have already seen it at its worst with toys everywhere and a kitchen covered in food, but knowing she'll be here soon means I want everything to be perfect. It's ridiculous because I know she's not coming to see the house, but I still can't stop myself.

I have the batter made and resting, every kind of topping I could find laid out on the table along with plates and drinks.

I've no idea what Leah did to Amelia yesterday, but she was still out for the count when I went up a few minutes ago to shower and dress.

My hands tremble around the coffee mug they're wrapped around as I wait. It's not just the anticipation of seeing Leah that I'm anxious about this morning. I've been keeping a secret from Amelia for months and today's the day I get to unveil all.

I'm wearing a pair of light blue cotton shorts. I've been told by my sister that they're a little on the tight side, so I thought they'd be perfect as I've caught Leah checking out my arse more than once, and a plain white t-shirt. I put way too much time into making sure my hair and beard were just so and I covered myself with my favourite aftershave. It cost so damn much that if she doesn't immediately drop to her knees I'll be bitterly disappointed.

The image that conjures up is just playing out in my mind, my cock swelling as if she were right in front of me when a light knock comes from the French doors.

Glancing up, my eyes immediately find her standing on the other side of the doors chewing on her bottom lip in uncertainty. Dropping my gaze, I take in the vest she's wearing that wraps around her body like a second skin and gives me a perfectly teasing hint of the full tits that hide beneath. Then on the bottom she's got on those damn hot pants that show off more than they hide.

Not able to stand the distance between us any longer, I push myself from the counter and head her way. Our eyes connect through the glass and hold.

Fumbling with the key, I groan in frustration that I didn't think to open it sooner so I could get to her easier. The second I pull the door open, I reach for her, wrap my hands around her waist and pull her to me. Her soft curves press up against my body and my semi hardens on contact.

"Fuck," I mutter before slamming my lips down on hers. I'm not at all gentle. Instead I put all the frustration I'm feeling about having to spend the night without her into it. I slip my tongue past her lips and she greedily sucks on it. Dropping my hands to her thighs, I lift her. Her legs wrap around my waist, lining my cock up with her centre perfectly.

"Jesus, fuck," I mutter, kissing across her jaw and down the soft skin of her neck.

"Jenson," she moans. "Where's Amelia?"

My chest swells that even at this moment she remembers my daughter. "Sleeping, so no screaming."

"Are you gonna...?" She trails off when I place her on the edge of the counter and continue to rock my length against her.

"Every time I see you, baby," I promise, my

mouth watering to take more than I'm going to be able to right now.

Dropping my lips to her chest, I kiss across the swell of her breasts before pulling the fabric of both her top and bra down so I can pull her hard nipple into my mouth. The taste of her fills my mouth making my cock weep for her.

Her chest heaves and she whimpers above me. Setting myself a challenge to see if I can get her off from this alone, I suck her deeper into my mouth once again before biting down.

The sound of her head hitting the cabinet behind her sounds out around us but when all she does is thread her fingers through my hair to keep me in place, I know it couldn't have hurt too badly.

Releasing her with a pop, I kiss and lick around her nipple before going to release her other breast to give it the same treatment.

"Jenson, please," she begs, spurring me on. But everything soon comes crashing down around us.

"Daddy, what are you doing to Leah?"

My eyes widen in shock and Leah gasps in horror as we both go to pull her top back up. Our hands collide in our haste, making the situation Amelia just walked into look even worse, I'm sure.

"Daddy?" I groan when I realise that she's not going to let this go without getting an answer.

"Leah fell into her bush."

Leah snorts at my excuse.

"I was just making sure she hadn't hurt herself. Are you ready for your pancakes, baby girl?"

I look over my shoulder just in time to see her huff out a breath of frustration at my use of the nickname she hates.

"Only if you stop calling me that."

"Not going to happen, so no pancakes for you."

"I didn't mean it, I didn't mean it," she says in a panic, rushing towards the table.

"I'm so sorry", I mouth to Leah as she slips down from the counter. My eyes flutter when she brushes against my length that's still threatening to break through the zip at any moment.

"You can make it up to me later, maybe?"

"Too fucking right."

"Amelia, would you like a drink?" Leah practically sings as she moves towards the table, leaving me feeling lost.

"Orange juice please. Daddy, what are you waiting for? Me and Leah are hungry, aren't we?"

"Uh... very hungry." Glancing over, her eyes find

mine. She might be hungry, but I know damn well it's not for my pancakes.

"I'll be back in just a few minutes to make them."

"Where are you going now?"

"Stop being so bossy, Amelia," I snap unintentionally. I feel awful when I turn to look and find her bottom lip trembling. "I'm sorry, I just need to... use the toilet."

Running from the room before my daughter spots what's going on below my waistband, I try to think of anything that will make it go down. Although I fear any progress I make will be ruined when I walk back into that room and see Leah again. She was so fucking close; if we hadn't been interrupted...

"You've been gone ages," Amelia helpfully points out when I walk back into the kitchen just a few minutes later much to Leah's amusement. Our eyes lock for a second before hers drop to my crotch, clearly wondering if I managed to fix my little—or not so—situation.

"Right, pancakes. Place your orders, girls."

"You okay?" Leah asks, coming to stand beside me as I pour some more batter into the pan.

"A little frustrated, but good. You?"

"I'm good. I'm sorry though. I shouldn't have allowed that to happen."

"It's not your fault and you do not need to apologise for it." Her eyebrow rises. "Okay, fine. It was kinda your fault. Have you seen yourself?"

Laughing, she playfully slaps my arm. "So, I thought you were going to teach me how to do this properly."

By the time we've used the last of the batter Leah is flipping pancakes like a pro.

"Did you see that? I did it! I flipped the perfect pancake."

"I told you it was easy."

"Yay," Amelia claps behind us. "You can come and cook me pancakes every morning now."

"Um... I'm not sure about that. I can't gate-crash every morning."

Leah's eyes flit to mine shyly and my heart drops. She doesn't think she belongs here, whereas I'm having fantasies about her sleeping in my bed and eating at this table with us on a daily basis, much like my daughter seems to be. It might be crazy after only a few days but already I can't picture my future without this woman in it.

"Let's just take each day as it comes, yeah?" Amelia's face drops whereas Leah's brows draw in

ANGEL DEVLIN & TRACY LORRAINE

with confusion. I hate that I've not made my intentions with her clear. It's something I need to rectify as soon as possible, even if it ends in her telling me that she has every intention of selling the house next door and moving on. I'd always regret not being honest with her about how I feel.

Placing the final plate of pancakes on the table, I quickly return to the kitchen and pull a present out from where I'd hidden it at the back of my pan drawer.

"What's that, Daddy?" Amelia asks excitedly, already bouncing on her chair to get a better look.

"Do you remember on your birthday I said I had one more present for you but that you'd have to wait?"

"Yes. What is it, what is it?"

Leah watches the exchange between us, her own curiosity getting the better of her as she leans in the second I place the gift in front of my daughter and watch her start ripping at the paper immediately.

"What is it?" Leah asks when Amelia lets out a delighted squeal.

"Thank you, Daddy. I've wanted a lightbox forever."

Leah's eyes find mine. They narrow, clearly

wondering why I kept something as simple as a lightbox back until today.

"Turn it over, baby girl."

"Oh my god, oh my god, oh my god," she screams once she's had a chance to read the message. "You're taking me to Disneyland?" Waiting to tell her that I'd booked this trip has been killing me. I've been desperate to see the look of wonder and excitement that's on her face right now, but I knew that if I did it too soon that her impatience would get the better of her. "Thank you," she squeals, launching herself at me from her chair. I just manage to catch her before she hits the floor.

Throwing her little arms around my shoulders, she holds me tightly and I'm reminded of why I'd do anything for my little girl. When Leah's eyes meet mine, I find them full of unshed tears. She knows how big this must be for Amelia. The sight of her emotion has a little of my own clogging my throat.

Eventually Amelia loosens her hold on me and I'm able to put her back on her feet so she can return to her abandoned pancakes.

She just goes to take a bite when she stills and looks up at me, her eyes wide as an idea hits her. "Is Leah coming too?"

"Uh…" I look between the hope on Amelia's face

and Leah's concerned one. An invite to join us is on the tip of my tongue when she beats me to it.

"I'm sorry, Amelia, but I can't. I'm too busy working on my house. Maybe another time."

"Aw, but can't you get someone else to do the house? I'm sure Daddy will pay for it, won't you Daddy?"

"You'll have an amazing time just the two of you. It'll be so much fun. Which princess do you want to see first?" And just like that Leah somehow manages to change the subject and puts a stop to me begging for her to come.

12

LEAH

I COULDN'T WAIT to get back around to Jenson's this morning and his welcome certainly didn't disappoint. Yet now, watching them together, chatting excitedly about Disneyland Paris just serves as a reminder that this is not my family. I spent the night dreaming they were, but she already has a mum, even if she's not around, and her father barely knows me.

It's only been a few days but I could see a lifetime with this man. Could see myself in a mother role to this girl, making that smile appear on her face and helping her with all the girly stuff. Maybe it's the fact I just lost my own parents that is making me throw myself among this small family? A reaction to loss? But it doesn't feel that way. It's bizarre, but I came back to my parents' home, walked next door and felt like I found mine.

My home.

I shake my head with the ridiculousness of my rambling brain. I'm now full of pancakes and Jenson and Amelia are talking about going swimming.

"Do you have a costume, Leah? Can you come?" Amelia's face is full of a hope I couldn't possibly dash.

"Sure. Give me half an hour?"

"Yaaayyyyy."

So my morning is spent in a pool where my time is split between encouraging Amelia with her doggy paddle and batting away Jenson's naughty underwater fingers.

"If you get dried off I'll take you to my restaurant for lunch." Jenson's cadence rises at the end of the sentence in a question. We're at the edge of the pool where his bottom half is pressing against me under the water while his face feigns innocence.

"Jesus. I'm still stuffed full of pancakes. You trying to make me the size of a house?"

"Nope. I just want to show off a little by showing you my restaurant, so indulge me." His eyes twinkle.

"Okay. I'd better go try and do something with my hair then." I say, moving my hand under the water and slipping it down the waistband of his swim shorts where I grasp him and pump my hand a few times. "Later, I'm going to sit on you and ride your dick so hard." I whisper in his ear. "Good luck getting out of the pool without looking like a dirty pervert." I giggle and I push myself out of the water.

There's a smack to my backside as I'm getting out.

I turn around, my eyes wide. "You did not just do that at a family pool."

Jenson smirks. "Shouldn't have been so naughty."

"What did she do, Daddy?" Amelia asks. "Did she say a naughty word?" She makes her way over to the edge near me.

"Leah, you must have been really, really naughty because Daddy has never smacked my bottom in my whole life."

"Yes, I was very naughty." I drop my gaze to Amelia. "I said some very bad words."

"We can still go for lunch though, right? Because I've been really good." Amelia pleads.

"Yes, if Leah promises to be a very good girl then we can still go for lunch, so do you promise to behave yourself, Leah?"

The urge to get back in the pool and put my

hand back down his shorts is almost overwhelming but instead I get up making sure my backside almost brushes his face.

"I'll be an absolute angel." I wink and then I make my way to the changing rooms.

———

INHALE IS a chic modern restaurant with shiny black floors, mirrored walls and square and rectangular dining tables with red tablecloths. The staff are all smart and are rushing around an extremely busy sitting.

"Hey, Boss. With you in a minute." A tall guy with chiselled cheekbones, deep dark doe-eyes, and arms I could swing off rushes past. I give him a second glance and Jenson notices, his chin tightening.

Oops.

"Is it always this busy?" I ask him.

"Yes, and it's going to get even busier soon. I'm about to be featured in The Sunday Times."

My jaw drops open. "Get out. You are not."

He stands up taller. "I am. And when women get a look at the hot guy that owns this place, they'll be flocking in droves."

My stomach tightens with an unrecognisable feeling. Is that jealousy?

"Hmmm, given the hot guy I just saw passing, I'd say you'd better extend the place to fit all the desperate women in."

I can feel the sparks flying between us and I'm surprised everyone else in the restaurant is oblivious to our teasing underlined by my fervent need to show him he's mine and no one else's by fucking him against one of the tables. His breaths are coming rapidly and I know he wants to smack my backside again right about now.

The guy comes back over.

"Uncle Scott. You said you'd come and be my prince and you have not been." Amelia yells at him.

He sweeps her up, those biceps pumping as he does so. I can't help it, I'm watching, and the thought it might be winding Jenson up too is just a bonus.

"You know me, Princess." Scott says. "Your Daddy keeps me locked up here like Rapunzel. I keep asking if I can go let down my hair and he says no. He's the wicked King keeping me trapped here in this restaurant palace. You need to free me, Princess Amelia." His voice is dramatic and Amelia giggles, no doubt used to this man's nonsense.

"Now, Amelia. You seem to have brought

another princess with you, so who is this one? Is this Jasmine?"

"No."

"Ariel?"

"No, silly."

"Oh, I know. It's Snow White."

"It's Princess Leah."

I see the flitter of amusement cross Scott's features.

"Leah, not Leia?"

"Lee-yah." I enunciate clearly.

The guy shrugs. "Huh, there goes my fantasies."

"Is there a table then, Scott?" Jenson's eyes are narrowed and he looks ready to kill Scott. In fact, if he could use the force I think Scott would be looking a little pained right now.

"Sure, follow me." He takes us to a quiet curtained-off corner and to a table set for four and then removes one set of cutlery. "I've not had lunch yet, but I take it I wouldn't be welcome." He's clearly teasing Jenson now.

He passes us a menu each which amuses me as Jenson no doubt knows every inch of it already.

"Anyone heard from Krissy yet?" Jenson asks, looking in the direction of the bar where a bartender is looking stressed as he's faced with a large queue.

"Nope. So I think we can safely say she's probably not coming back."

"I'll get on it first thing in the morning. We're off to Disneyland on Wednesday. I'll make sure you have someone by then."

Scott nods and moves away, saying he'll be back to take our orders.

"What's that all about?" I ask him.

"One of our regular bar staff seems to have quit without actually telling us. We're too busy to be short staffed. I don't like anything that gives customers a cause for complaint."

I stand up and Jenson's brow creases. "What are you doing?"

"Order me a lasagne. I bartended my way through college. I'll go help clear the queue."

"I can't ask you to do that."

"You aren't asking and I'm only doing it now just to help that poor guy out. He looks like he wants to cry. I'll be back by the time my food is served. Then you can ring round your staff to get the evening covered or I'll stay. But tomorrow you're on your own because I have a house to fix up."

With that I saunter over to the bar, chat to Chester and ask if he wants a hand and away we go.

Fifteen minutes later Chester thinks I'm an angel sent from heaven and I'm tucking into my lasagne.

"You're becoming a little indispensable to me." Jenson whispers in my ear, making shivers run from my lobe down my spine. "I'm going to miss you when we're in Disney. Sure you can't come?"

"Not to Disney, but I can *come.*" I whisper back. "I think you're going to need to make sure I'm highly satisfied if I have to survive until Sunday evening before you return."

"I intend to make sure of that," he whispers darkly.

"It's rude to whisper. That's what you tell me, Daddy. I can't hear what you're saying to each other."

"Oh it's a secret about Disney, Princess."

"Sweet! Okay then. Can I have some ice cream?"

"How is your daughter not sixty stone?" I ask Jenson.

The answer becomes clear once Amelia is full of food as she hurtles around the restaurant until Jenson scoops her up and says we need to leave because she's going to annoy the customers. He's managed to get bar cover for the evening, so with that in mind we make our way home.

Once Amelia has run around like something

possessed for several more hours, she makes her way to bed and then after so do we. I once more get escorted around to my own property in the early hours.

"When I get back from Disney, you're staying, even if I have to buy that house myself, to force you out of it." Jenson groans cupping my breast. "It's no good," he says and pulls me around the side of the house.

"What are you doing?" I shriek as Jenson pushes me against the bricks. He unfastens my jeans and pulls them past my knees, then moves my panties to the side with deft fingers and slips first one, then another inside my slick opening.

"I'm becoming addicted to feeling you explode around me," he growls in my ear. My eyes flutter closed. There are people talking in the distance, people who could walk past the house at any moment and potentially see what's happening. The thought of being discovered just makes things ten times hotter. I thrust my hips up to meet his fingers. He curls them inside me in just the right way that within minutes I'm gasping as my body trembles and my core pulses around his fingers.

"Oh God, Oh God." My exaltations are captured in his mouth as he feasts on my lips. Dropping to my knees, I open the waistband of his trousers and pull those and his pants down, freeing his erect cock. Gripping him firmly at the base, I take him in my mouth.

Jenson's hands come to the back of my head and one fist wraps firmly around a clutch of my hair. As he gets more excited, he guides my head, showing me just how he likes it. I tongue the end of his glans and then deep throat him until with a, "Fuck, Leah," his balls tighten and he releases his sticky, salty load into my mouth. I swallow everything he has to give.

Eventually he manages to walk me to my door and says goodnight.

THE NEXT MORNING I'm actually up bright and early. I'd refused the offer of breakfast as I had Carl starting early this morning as he wanted to try to get the dining room and the bathroom plastered today.

As he walks in the door, he takes in my beaming smile. "Someone's had a good weekend then. Either that or you've accidentally sat on a cucumber?"

"Carl!" I laugh. "Is that any way to talk to someone employing you?"

"Smiling looks good on you," he says. "You coming out with us again on Friday?"

"Erm, yeah, sure."

"You can ditch us for cock if you need to."

"I'm not having this conversation." I laugh. "Do you talk to all women like this?"

"Only ones I know are okay with banter. Like my cousin."

"The bartender?"

"Yeah. Well, she was. Until she got sacked for telling the boss to go fuck himself. Got a bit of sass has my cous."

Synapses fire in my brain. "She looking for another job? I can't promise but I know someone who's looking. She will have to rein it in though, it's a classy establishment."

"Er, maybe."

"I'll be putting the kettle on, you call her."

By the time I put a steaming hot cuppa in Carl's hands he has a mobile number for his cousin for me.

I text it to Jenson.

Me: My plasterer's cousin is a recently

sacked bartender. She's sassy but cute. She'll bring all the boys to the yard.

MY PHONE PINGS A MINUTE LATER.

Jenson: Leah to the rescue. I'll have to find a way to say thank you... when will I see you?

Me: Later. I need to get on or this house will never be finished.

Jenson: I don't want it to ever be finished...

I STARE AT HIS MESSAGE. At the three little dots at the end. And I wonder what is going to happen. It's likely that by the time he and Amelia are back from Disney, the house will be ready for the market, and I will be free to leave.

But I don't want to go.

Frustration that I have to sell, that this can't be my home because of unscrupulous loan sharks has me punching the sofa. I'll be lucky if I'm left with enough to buy a keyring with, never mind a house. I need to start looking for a job shortly.

I need a bloody miracle, and some more paint.

13

JENSON

"HEY, HOW WAS YOUR WEEKEND?" I ask Kaylie when she eventually picks up the phone.

"Ugh, disaster."

"So you didn't get a guy to take you home and show you a good time then?" I cringe asking the question, but I just want her to be happy.

"No, Aiden brought me home because I was too pissed to even stand up."

Aiden is her best friend. They've been close since we were all kids. Everyone's always thought they were perfect for each other but still all these years on nothing's happened between them, well not that I know of.

"And he didn't even kiss you goodnight?"

"No, Jenson. He didn't," she snaps.

"Fine, listen, I need a favour."

"Of course you do."

"This is the last one for a while because we're off to Disney on Wednesday but there's something I've got to do before we go."

"Go on..."

"I've met someone... I think."

"Oooh give me the details." I hear rustling down the line and I smile knowing she's ready to hear all the gossip.

"Maybe later. But is there any chance you could stay a little later tonight so I could take her out?" Kaylie was already booked in to look after Amelia so I could pop into work this afternoon. A few extra hours shouldn't hurt so I could take Leah out, right?

"Fine. But you owe me."

"When don't I?" I ask with a chuckle.

"Where are you taking her?"

"No idea. That was going to be my next question."

With a sigh, Kaylie starts rattling ideas off for the perfect date with Leah. It's even more proof that she needs a man if she's got a million dates planned in her head.

Her suggestions do give me some ideas and after making sure Amelia is okay playing in the living room, I quickly pop next door.

It takes her a little too long to come to the door and when she does eventually pull it open looking hot and flustered, my fists clench with frustration—or maybe it's jealousy, I'm not sure. It was obvious the minute I walked out of the house that she wasn't alone because that damn van was parked in the driveway once again.

"Hey, I'm sorry, Carl was just—"

"Carl was just what?" My voice comes out as a growl, making Leah's eyes narrow.

Her hands land on her hips as she blows out a frustrated breath. "Banging me against the wall." Her eyes roll dramatically telling me she's joking but my heart starts to race nonetheless.

"Short stack, where have you gone? I can't hold this curtain pole up all fucking day."

Leah's head tilts to the side as she waits to see what I'm going to do. Knowing she's alone with him has been infuriating at the best of times but right now I want to go and grab Amelia, put on our painting clothes and insist we help, to ensure he keeps his hands to himself.

Tension crackles between us, the silence stretching out a little too long. Eventually we're interrupted by a crash from somewhere in the house. "Fucking hell, that's your fault, shortie."

Shaking her head, her eyes continue to hold mine. "Did you need something, only we're kinda busy?" She knows exactly what she's doing and her small smirk ensures I'm aware.

"Uh... yeah. Are you free tonight?"

"I can be. Why?"

"Kaylie is babysitting and I want to take you out."

"Like on a real date?"

"Yeah, if you're up for it."

"I'm up for it."

"Good, I'll pick you up about seven."

Rushing back towards my house, I poke my head into the living room to find Amelia exactly where I left her with her dolls.

"You want some lunch, baby girl?"

"Yes please, Daddy," she calls without even looking up from what she's doing.

I END up running late at the restaurant and come rushing through the house, shouting a hello to Amelia and Kaylie as I run up the stairs to get ready for my date. Even thinking the word makes me feel a little weird. I haven't had a date in years. But I don't ever remember being this nervous.

I jump in and out of the shower. I'm barely in there long enough to get wet before I pull on a pair of dark jeans and a slim white t-shirt. Throwing some wax through my hair and rubbing some oil into my beard, I stand back and look at the result.

"You look handsome, Daddy. Just like a real-life prince."

"Aw, thank you, baby. Have you been a good girl today?"

"Of course I have."

"Good girl. I'm sorry I can't read your story tonight, but I've got to go out."

"It's okay. I hope you and Leah have a good night."

My mouth drops open a little. "How'd you know I'm going out with Leah?"

"I guessed."

Turning to look at her, she squirms under my stare. "Really?"

"No, she overheard me talking to Mum on the

phone," Kaylie confesses as we make it to her in the kitchen.

"Amelia, what have I told you about eavesdropping?"

"I'm sorry, Daddy. But Aunt Kaylie was talking so loud I couldn't help but hear." Giving my sister a death stare, I go to collect the flowers I dropped on the counter as I rushed in. "How old is Leah, Daddy? Aunt Kaylie said she's very young."

"Really?" I snap at my sister.

"Sorry," she mouths but it's too late. I'm irritated. I don't know how many times I've told her that Amelia listens to everything these days and will repeat it given the opportunity.

"Try to be good tonight."

"I will," Amelia sings.

"I meant Aunt Kaylie." I pin my sister with another look before turning, giving Amelia a kiss and marching from the house.

"Hey," Leah, says pulling the door open soon after I've knocked. I don't give myself a chance to check her out; I'm too desperate for her.

My palm lands on her cheek, my eyes staring deep into her light blue ones as I step inside and push her back against the wall. My lips slam down on hers and I take what I've been desperate for since our little session down the side of her house last night. Hitching her leg up around my waist, I press my already hard cock against her.

Her moans of pleasure fill the space around us, and they're soon joined by my own growl as her hands slip up inside my t-shirt and her nails scratch across her back.

My tongue plunges into her mouth, exploring her like it's our first kiss.

Once I've managed to clear some of the frustration today has filled me with, I step back.

"Wow, that was some welcome."

"Couldn't help myself." My eyes drop from hers and I do what I should have done when she first opened the door. "You look beautiful." She's wearing a pink, floral sundress which shows off her incredible cleavage and sits high on her thighs.

"Thank you." A shy little smile forms on her lips and fuck if I don't want to pin her back to the wall again. "You don't look too bad yourself. So are we going out or did you want to...?" She gestures over her shoulder. Glancing to the hallway behind her, my muscles ache to do as she suggests and spend our first date inside her. But that's not what tonight is meant to be about.

I want to treat her properly. To show her what

being with me could be like aside from being a parent to Amelia. We haven't exactly had the conventional start to whatever this is, so I want to do something right.

"No, we're going out."

"Okay, let me grab my bag."

Stepping from the house, I wait for her to lock up before leading her towards my car with my hand resting in the small of her back.

We chat about the restaurant and her renovations as we head into town. I explain how I'm interviewing her bartender suggestion first thing in the morning and she tells me a little more about her. I'm not all that thrilled that she's connected with her workman, but beggars can't be choosers.

"You're taking me bowling?" she guesses correctly as I pull up a little way down the street from the bowling alley.

"Yeah, I thought it would be fun."

"I'm not exactly dressed for it."

"You'll be fine. Come on." I intend to be a gentleman and open her door for her but by the time I get around the car she's already standing on the pavement waiting for me.

Threading my fingers through hers, we walk into the building and book a lane.

It's not until she goes to do her first throw that I start to understand why she was concerned about what she's wearing. Rearing her arm back, she steps forward and throws, but no one's eyes are on the bowled ball as it speeds off down the lane because her shapely legs, and more importantly her arse, are almost on full display to every motherfucker in this place.

With my muscles locked tight, I push from the bench I was sitting on and storm over.

"We're leaving."

"What. Why?"

"You were right. You're not dressed for this."

Her eyes flick over my face, an amused smile appearing on her lips.

"Wow," she breathes.

"What?"

"I didn't have you down as one to go all alpha caveman on me."

"Leah," I sigh, exasperated with her amusement. "You just showed every man in this place how tiny that little G-string is you're wearing and now every single one of them is imagining fucking you."

She glances over my shoulder and shifts her eyes around the room.

"No one's even looking this way."

"Trust me, they were. And they will be again if you bend over like that. Come on." I go to pull her away from the lane and get her the hell out of here but she holds firm.

"We've only just started. I promise not to bend over so much, how's that?"

My teeth grind as I picture just how much she put on show for everyone to see only seconds ago. Can I sit here and allow her to do it all over again? Leah's standing with her hands on her hips and a defiant look on her face.

"Do I have a choice?"

"Not really."

"Fucking hell."

Her hands land on my chest and she pushes until I'm forced to fall back down onto the bench and watch.

By the time she takes her last go, beating me by a mile, I'm just about ready to explode. A group of young guys took over the next lane to us about twenty minutes ago and I know every single one of them stops to watch every time Leah takes to the lane. I didn't need to turn to acknowledge it, their sudden silence said it all.

"I can't believe I won," Leah squeals as we leave, hand in hand.

"I was distracted."

"Oh come on. What's the big deal? So what? I showed off a little more than I was planning to. I'm leaving with you, aren't I? And if you're a lucky boy I might show you my bedroom later."

"Yeah?"

"Only time will tell. What's next? I'm starving."

Getting back into the car, I take us a little out of the city to an event Kaylie told me about.

"What's this?" Leah asks, her brows drawn together as I pull up into the car park and get out, retrieving a box and blanket from the boot.

"I'm not totally sure. My sister recommended it."

"Okay, well lead the way."

We follow the path and eventually emerge from the trees to find a huge field with people scattered around sitting on their own blankets and enjoying their own picnics as a band play on the makeshift stage at the other side of the park.

We find a patch of grass and I lay the blanket out before opening up the basket and excitedly pull out all the dishes I prepared earlier.

"Did you make all of this?" Leah asks, staring down at it all in amazement.

"Yep, with my very own magic hands."

"I'll be interested to see what else you're going to do with those magic hands later." She purrs.

I put the food down and we make out on the blanket until I hear her tummy gurgle. We eat and then she says the words I've waited to hear all night.

"Do you want to come back to mine?"

14

LEAH

THE CAR JOURNEY home can't pass fast enough. I'm desperate for him to be inside me. A quick phone call to his sister and he had permission to be out all night. Kaylie was staying over anyway and she said it would be nice to enjoy a quiet night with all the gorgeous leftovers in Jenson's fridge.

The minute we're through the door, Jenson grabs my hand and begins to drag me up the stairs. "Which way?"

"To the top and to the right. My bedroom is over the back garden."

I wish he could have seen the house as it used to be, full of life like his. Instead, the essence of the house has been stripped away. It's a blank canvas for its next owner, or it will be when I'm finished.

Thank goodness I'd tidied all my crap away thinking this could be a possibility. There are freshly laundered sheets on my bed. Not that Jenson seems to have taken in any of it: not the bare walls, not the room. He's completely engaged in the moment and I realise I should be too. Not worrying about what he thinks of my home!

I wrap my legs around him and clutching my arse cheeks he lowers me onto my bed, rolling me over and lifting my dress to expose my G-string.

"This arse is mine, you hear me? Not all the dudes at Bowl Me Overs." He bites each cheek in turn.

"Oh my god. Seriously? You just bit my arse and claimed it? What a Neanderthal."

He flips me back over and beats at his chest. "Woman, mine."

I sit up, reach over and tug at the end of his shirt. "You're wearing far too many clothes, Jenson Hale."

It's not long before we're wearing nothing at all.

Jenson nibbles at my neck, trailing tiny kisses the whole way down, sweeping across my collarbone, to the other side of my neck. I shiver, goose bumps erupting everywhere. He teases my nipples in turn and then trails down further and further until his mouth is feasting between my thighs and I'm screaming his name.

When he finally enters me, his gaze is fixed on my own. "Keep your eyes open." He orders as he thrusts deep inside me.

"It's hard." I complain, my eyes wanting to close to experience all the heady sensations.

"Oh I know," he quips.

In revenge I swirl my hips a little taking him deeper.

"Fuck, Leah. I can't get enough of you."

A fact he proves by us getting very little sleep until a resounding knock comes on the wall.

"For God's sake, quit shagging." A female voice booms out.

"Oh shit. Your own spare room adjoins this one. Please tell me your sister hasn't been listening to us banging all night," I say mortified, hiding my face in his chest. Mmm, it smells all spicy. I lick his sweaty, salty skin.

"Now stop that or I'll scar my sister mentally for life." He chuckles in my ear. Then gathering me into his warm embrace, he tucks my head underneath his chin and we fall asleep until my regular set alarm lets us know that it's morning.

"I AM NOT GOING AROUND to meet your sister." I fold my arms over my chest.

"Please yourself. I know Kaylie. She'll just come around here."

"What?"

Jenson shrugs. "There's been no woman in my life, no regular woman that is, since my ex. She's very protective of Amelia and she'll want to give you the once-over."

"This just gets better and better." I groan.

After showering, I change into a pair of navy trousers and a white blouse. Jenson looks at me strangely. "Can I voice an objection? Where are the itty-bitty shorts?"

"Objection overruled. I'm meeting your sister. I'm not going around in my paint-splattered decorating attire."

"Well, can I put in a request that you wear it tonight? Can I dip my brush in your paint pot?"

The doorbell rings.

"That'll be Carl."

I'm expecting Jenson to go all alpha again, but instead he just says nothing while I go downstairs to let him in.

"Morning, short stack. Can't smell any tea. Can't work unless I have my fill of the hot stuff."

A deep voice booms from behind me. "Me too. Sorry, that's why she's running behind."

I'll kill him. I feel my face burn.

Carl guffaws and making his way through the door he sidesteps me to hold out a hand to Jenson which is met and shaken. "Carl Taylor. Plasterer and Building Services. Though you'll know that if you've eyes because it's sign-written on my van. Just want to say thanks, mate, for interviewing my cousin today. Means a lot. Found out the reason she lost her job was her ex-boss was hitting on her. Least I know that won't be happening in your place. Seems you're otherwise engaged." He tilts his head at me.

"Shit, yes, the interview. I need to get back to mine and get ready. You coming?" he asks me.

I now have the perfect excuse not to go. "Nah, I need to make this needy guy a gallon of tea."

"My sister won't be happy."

"Sister?" Carl asks.

"Yeah, she's looking after my daughter. She'll want to meet this one."

"Well, just so happens I have a flask of tea in the van and also I do know how to use a kettle, so bye, Leah. Get out from under my feet, will you? Bloody distracting seeing you looking like you're going for a job interview. I'm missing the shorts."

A mini growl erupts from Jenson.

Carl winks at him. "I'm a hot-blooded male. You might be tapping it, but I'm not blind."

"Yeah, those shorts are really something aren't they?"

"Oh my god, you seriously are not talking about me in this way." I stomp my feet and head out of the front door.

I can hear Jenson still laughing behind me.

"Stop stomping. You look like Amelia when she can't get her own way."

I swing around at him. "You'll be getting none tonight."

His smile is delicious and flames lick up my insides. "But that's not true is it? Because I go to Disney tomorrow, so I think you'll want to ride me all night long."

I laugh out loud and he looks confused for a moment until he turns around to face his sister standing at the opened door.

"I'm going to vomit. Right here on the step. Vomit everywhere. Can you please stop?" She smiles at me. "Leah, right?"

I nod, blushing furiously once more.

"Come in. Amelia's just run upstairs to get changed as I bought her a new Rapunzel dressing up outfit."

As we follow Kaylie through to the kitchen, she's chattering about how fast Amelia is growing and how she doesn't think this outfit will last that long either before she's either grown out of it or got bored of Disney princesses.

"As long as she doesn't get bored of them before tomorrow."

"You're joking, Jenson. She's talked of nothing else. Actually, that's not true." Kaylie pauses and turns to look at me then her brother. "She talked an awful lot about Leah too. Apparently, you've been filling Leah's holes." She raises her brows a few times in an 'oo-er' kind of way. "I'm presuming she's not been witnessing things she shouldn't."

"He helped me plant some trees in the front garden." I scrub at my hair. "Oh God, what a first impression I must be making."

To my surprise Kaylie walks up to me and gives me a hug. She's a good half a foot taller than I am so the sunlight disappears for a moment.

"It's a pleasure to meet the woman who is putting a smile back on my brother's face." She lets me go and heads back to the countertop. "Coffee or tea?"

"Coffee please. I can't stay long though, I have the plasterer next door, and a carpet fitter coming."

"How long before it's ready for sale?"

"I'm expecting to be able to call the estate agents early next week."

I can see Jenson's body tense at my response.

Kaylie places a coffee on the table for all three of us and we take a seat. "So then what?"

"Kaylie! That's not our business." Jenson warns.

"It's okay." I tell him. "Then, I don't know." I decide to confess all. "My parents got into debt with con artists. You know those firms who tell you they'll release you your equity? They signed a loan agreement without reading the fine print. I have to sell the house to cover what they owe. I'll be lucky if there's anything left for even a deposit on anything else. So, I need to look for a job and depending on what I get, then I'll look for a rental. I'm stuck really until the house is sold. I don't want to leave it vacant because I can't afford for anything to go wrong like squatters or burglars."

"Why haven't you told me any of this?" Jenson snaps.

"I haven't really wanted to face it." I say

honestly, but now it's coming towards the end of the refurb, and soon I'll be able to draw a line under it all.

"So what sort of work are you looking for? I'm sure Jenson will have something for you at InHale."

"I have an Early Years degree. But of course all the teaching posts for the new academic year will no doubt be filled now. Like I said, I'm a little stuck until the house sells, but I'll probably see if I can get a temporary teaching assistant position."

"I'm a primary school teacher!" Kaylie almost shouts.

"Really?"

"Yeah. I'll ask the head when I'm back, see if we have anything coming up."

"I'd really appreciate that."

"Daaddddyyyyyy. I need you to be the prince please." Amelia stands in the doorway dressed as Rapunzel, swishing her long wig.

"Rapunzel, Rapunzel, let down your hair."

Amelia giggles and runs in throwing herself into Jenson's arms.

"Well, do you know where Amelia is, Princess Rapunzel, because I want to say goodbye to her before I go to work?"

Amelia pulls her wig off. "It's me, Daddy, silly."

"Oh gosh, so it is."

"You look beautiful as Rapunzel, Amelia." I tell her.

"Thanks, Leah. Did you and my daddy have a sleepover?"

"Erm..."

"Did you tell ghost stories? That's what happened when I stayed over at Tasha Jenkins' house. Her big brother came in and told us a ghost story and we didn't sleep all night."

"I think Daddy must have told Leah ghost stories because they didn't sleep all night either." Kaylie says in an innocent voice while smirking.

"Right, I'm off to get ready for work. I'll leave you three to it." Jenson swallows down his coffee and swings Amelia around, placing her on the seat he's just got up from.

I watch as he leaves the room. Now I feel really awkward.

"So, Amelia. What are you having for breakfast today?" Kaylie asks her.

"Pancakes please."

Kaylie shakes her head. "Nope, not today. I know you've been having pancakes all week."

"But I love pancakes."

"You need some vitamins. What about porridge with sliced apple?"

"Oooooh, nooooooo. I want pancakes. Leah, make me pancakes."

Way to put me in an awkward spot.

"I think the eggs have run out, Amelia. So maybe the porridge, or some toast?"

"There's a shop down the street. Let's go buy some more."

I can see Kaylie's exasperation.

"Maybe, I could go get some?" I say quietly.

"No. She needs to learn she can't have her own way all the time." Kaylie snaps.

"God, yeah. I guess so. I don't really know about her diet..." I trail off. In the meantime, Amelia has run up to her bedroom saying she's not eating at all.

"I'm sorry." Kaylie says. "I'm just trying to be someone who shows Amelia she can't always have things her own way. Jenson spoils her. I mean he's bound to and well, to a large extent, so do I, but I just want to make sure she's not living on sugar every morning."

"But your brother is a chef, surely he knows her nutritional needs?"

Kaylie slumps.

"God, you must think I'm such a bitch. I'll go get

some eggs. Can you watch Amelia? I think I'm just having a bit of a moment." Her eyes fill with tears. I jump from my seat and walk around to her.

"Is everything okay?"

She nods, but tears roll down her cheeks. "I'm so happy Jenson has met you. I know it's really early days but it just reminds me of how alone I am. I'm Amelia's auntie but I know I'm going to have to step back at some time, that a woman will come and take on the mother role that I've been doing my best to cover as her aunt. God, I'm talking shit I know. I'm so sorry. This wasn't how I wanted to introduce myself."

I walk over to the side and pass her a piece of kitchen towel.

"Kaylie, I've known Jenson less than two weeks."

"I know." She sniffles, "But I can just tell that this is different."

"Kaylie. I like your brother a lot, but it's two weeks. Next week my house will be going up for sale and then I have no idea what's going to happen. I might get a job in another city. Plus Amelia is always going to need her auntie."

Kaylie nods.

"Now, go and deal with Amelia and you're right, she does need to know she can't have her own way all the time. I'm going to leave you to it and get back to the house, okay?"

"I'm sorry, Leah."

"Don't be sorry for fearing change. I'm right there with you. In a few weeks time I could be anywhere."

"You're planning to leave?"

I spin around to see Jenson in his work clothes with Amelia on his back. She's forgotten her tantrum and is beaming at being on her dad's shoulders. Jenson's face however looks like an approaching thunderstorm.

"I don't know." I shrug my shoulders. I can only be honest. "Right, I'll catch you all later." This morning has proved all kinds of awkward and to be honest right now I can't cope. It's enough I have all this crap with my parents' estate on my plate. I can't be doing with a man I've had a few dates with's bad mood, his sister's meltdown, and Amelia's tantrums. It's just all too much. Grabbing my keys off the table, I walk out of the house and back to my own, where I let Carl's banter distract me.

15

JENSON

AS I SIT at my desk waiting for my potential new barmaid to arrive for her interview, Leah's words about leaving from earlier are on repeat in my head. Would she really up and leave after what's been between us?

It makes me wonder if I'm more invested in what's developing between us than she is. I guess it's only natural seeing as I'm so much older than her. She has every right not to be thinking about the potential to become Amelia's stepmum and here I am having crazy thoughts about her being just that.

"Jesus," I mutter dropping my head into my hands. I've known her what, a week, and here I am thinking about marriage and a future.

A knock sounds out, dragging my head back up

and distracting me from my crazy thoughts. "She's perfect," Scott says, sticking his head into my office without being invited.

"So by that you mean you want to bang her?"

"Yeah! So will you when you see her."

"Doubtful," I mutter quietly, but apparently it's not quite quietly enough.

"Ah, I forgot. You've already got yourself a hot and young piece of ass."

Fire burns through my veins at him even mentioning Leah after the way he shamelessly flirted with her in front of me. Reaching out, I grab his arm and pull him back until he hits the wall. "Don't ever let me hear you talk about Leah like that again."

Wide, panic filled eyes stare back at me. "Shit, I'm so sorry, Boss."

"I should fucking fire you. You're a pain in my arse."

He smiles at me and I'm sure it would get him far with a horny woman, but me, not so much. "Just think of all the female customers you'd lose without me."

I refrain from pointing out that they probably come here for the food. I don't want to bruise his ego.

"She's by the bar," he calls from behind me. "But

I've already called dibs."

Shaking my head, I walk out into the restaurant to find a petite dark-haired woman sitting on one of the bar stools.

"Hi, you must be Suki?" I ask as I approach. Spinning on the stool, she jumps down and holds her hand out for me.

"Yes, that's me."

It takes me a second to respond because even though Scott just pointed out how hot she was, and Leah said something about her getting all the guys in, I'm still slightly taken aback by just how beautiful she is. Her dark hair frames her face perfectly, her dark eye make-up makes her brown eyes look like melted chocolate and her red lips... well I don't really need to go there because I've got Leah and although beautiful, this woman isn't really my type. I think Leah described her as sassy; well in person she looks way more than sassy. I think she could probably eat most men alive. If Scott wants to try his luck then fair play to him, he needs someone to keep him on his toes.

"Would you like to come through?"

Turns out, I don't think I could have found anyone more perfect for the job and before the interview's over, I make her an offer she can't refuse.

Thankfully, she agrees to start immediately, meaning I can head off to Disney and not worry about staffing issues.

By the time I leave for the day, ensuring that the place will run like a well-oiled machine without me, excitement flutters in my stomach. I've wanted to take Amelia to Disneyland since the day she watched her very first Disney film. The anticipation of the look on her face when she sees that castle is enough to have emotion clogging my throat.

She's already in her pyjamas when I walk through the front door.

"If you think she's going to sleep tonight you're fooling yourself," my sister warns.

Amelia races towards me screaming. "I'm going to Disneyland tomorrow."

"It might be one of the reasons I didn't mention it when I booked it. I couldn't cope with months of this."

"It'll be amazing. I'm jealous."

"You'll get to take your own kids there one day, Kay."

"Hopefully." The sadness in her voice is enough to make me change the subject.

"Any plans while I'm gone?"

"Er, going out with Aiden tomorrow night. Then

out with the girls on Friday night; it's Cheryl's birthday."

"Sounds like fun."

"Should be." There's not a lot of enthusiasm in her voice and my heart aches for her. She's so desperate to find the one and spend her life with someone. "All of your washing is done and folded on your beds. I wasn't sure what you wanted Amelia to take so I didn't pack for you."

"Kay, you didn't need to do all of that."

"You know I like to keep busy."

"Have you eaten?"

"Yeah, I had pasta with Amelia. I'm just going to head off if that's okay. Leave you to get sorted."

Pulling my sister in for a hug, I wish there was something I could do, but as usual, I come up short with ideas.

"Amelia, come and say goodbye to Auntie Kaylie, please." Her footsteps thunder our way and I leave them to do their thing as I head upstairs to start packing.

I'm deep in thought trying to decide which of Amelia's dresses to pack when she shouts up the stairs.

"Daddy, Leah's here." My heart jumps into my throat. I've got plans for tonight, so my daughter had better get tired soon. Throwing her favourite dresses into her small case, I zip it up and leave it in the corner of her room with a change of clothes on top ready for the morning. In order to catch our train we've got to leave at ridiculous o'clock. Even more reason why she needs to get to bed.

Jogging down the stairs, I round the corner into the kitchen and find the two of them sitting at the table with a glass of milk each.

"Leah warmed mine up. She says it'll make me sleepy, but I've already told her that I'm not going to bed tonight. I'm staying awake until we need to leave."

Leah winks at me and my cock swells. I'm glad she's got similar plans for the night.

"You need to sleep tonight, Amelia. I read that the princesses refuse to see naughty children." Her eyes widen and she quickly reaches for her milk and downs it.

"Okay. I'm going to bed right now. Make sure you tell them that I was extra good."

I watch in amazement as she hops from the chair and runs for the stairs.

"Well, that was easier than I was expecting."

"Blackmail always works," Leah says with a laugh.

"So I guess you're here for dinner?"

"Yeah, that and something else."

"How hungry are you?"

"For food, meh. For you... fucking starved." Her fist wraps around my shirt and I let her pull me towards her. Reaching up on her tiptoes, she whispers in my ear, "how quickly do you think she's going to fall asleep?"

"I hope fast because I've had this fantasy about fucking you on this table."

"This table?" she asks, stepping away from me and running her fingertip along the edge of the wood.

"Yeah, that one."

"How would you want me? Bent over like this?" I just about manage to contain my groan when she bends over and sticks her arse out. Her skirt rises and I get a flash of the hot pink G-string she's wearing. "Or like this?" Turning, she hops up onto the table and spreads her legs wide giving me one fucking incredible view. Her chest heaves as she waits to see what I'm going to do and my mouth waters with my need to taste her.

Dropping to my knees, I pull the small scrap of fabric to the side and run my tongue up the length of her.

"Oh fuck," she whimpers above me, her feet coming to rest on my shoulders.

"Shhh."

Pushing forward, I eat her until she's thrashing about on top of the table and coming all over my face.

Sitting back, I wipe my mouth with the back of my hand. A smug smile spreads across my lips when I look at her laid back on the table, her tits rising and falling with her increased breaths and a light sheen of sweat over her face and chest.

"Ready for more?"

"Like you wouldn't believe."

Popping open the buttons on my jeans, I push both them and my boxers down my thighs. Taking my length in my hand, I run the head through her wet folds enjoying the feeling of her trembling.

"Jenson, please."

I'm just about to thrust into her when I realise something. "Condoms are upstairs."

"I'm on birth control. We're good."

"I'm clean, I swear."

"Me too. Do it."

Unable to deny her, I thrust forward. The intense feeling of her wrapped around me is enough to make my movement still for a second. My heart thunders in my chest as I look down at the incredible woman beneath me. This is all going so fast but I never want it to fucking stop.

"Fuck," I grunt. "Do you feel that?"

"Yes. More, more."

The feeling of our bodies connecting with nothing between us was only part of what I meant. I just fucking hope she feels the swelling inside her chest as well because I'm not sure how I'll cope if she doesn't.

Pulling her tiny body over the edge, I hold her arse in my hands and shift her so she's at the perfect angle. Her pussy squeezes me tight and I know she's just about to crash over the edge.

"Don't scream."

"Fuuuck, Jenson," she moans, her hands lifting to squeeze her tits. Fuck, I wish she was naked right now so I could watch her playing with her own nipples. The thought alone has my cock swelling as my balls draw up.

"Come now, Leah," I demand, pressing my thumb down on her sensitive clit.

"Shit, Jenson," she cries, unable to help herself as she falls apart beneath me.

"Leah, fuck," I moan, following her over the edge.

Dropping her legs to the floor, I help her stand before tucking myself back inside my trousers. "You hungry for food now?"

"Not really. Fancy taking this upstairs? I could really use a shower after that."

Dropping my eyes, I run them over her curves trying to imagine how fucking sexy they'll look with water running over them.

"Me too. I'm dirty as fuck."

"I know."

Reaching out, she grabs my hand and together we run up the stairs laughing like bloody teenagers.

***

IT'S STILL DARK when my alarm goes off. I quickly grab my phone from the side and turn it off so I don't wake Leah. Slipping from the bed, I grab the clothes I left out before she got here last night and tug them on as silently as possible.

It takes a couple of minutes to get Amelia to wake up enough to remember why I'm waking her in the middle of the night.

"We're going to Disney," she screams, jumping out of bed and running around like a lunatic.

"Shhhh."

"Why? I'm so excited."

"I know, baby, but Leah's asleep in the other room."

"You had another sleepover, Daddy? I'm glad you didn't tell her scary stories all night and keep her awake."

Oh I kept her awake all right.

Come on, you need to get dressed. We need to be out of the house in ten minutes.

I leave Amelia to get dressed and brush her teeth while I take our cases downstairs and write a note for Leah.

Grabbing the spare key, I take it and the note upstairs and place it on the bedside table next to where she's sleeping. I drop a quick kiss on her forehead and sneak from the room, wishing the whole time that she was coming with us.

"Are you ready?" I ask when I find Amelia at the front door next to the cases with a princess doll under each arm.

"Yes, let's go already."

I glance up at my bedroom window as we head down the driveway. Is it wrong of me to hope something goes wrong with her house so it's not ready to be sold next week? I'm not ready for her to go yet.

16

LEAH

I WAKE WONDERING where I am. Then realisation slams into me that I'm in Jenson's bed as his spicy smell hits my nostrils. I reach out my arm but meet cold sheets.

What?

Sitting up quickly, I see that I'm alone. He and Amelia have gone on their trip. I spot the note on the bedside table and a key.

Leah,
You looked far too content to wake up.
Here's the spare key.
Stay as long as you like. Feel free to stay

here while we're away and eat anything left in the fridge!
I've not left yet and I'm already missing you.
J x

I RUN my fingers over his words. Stay as long as I like. I think I'd quite like to stay forever. God, he'd think I was a nutcase if I said that to him after these few days together.

I feel a pang in my chest at the thought I won't see him or Amelia for five days. Sunday evening is a long way off.

It feels strange being in the house without them, so I hurry to leave and get back to my parents' house. Today I intend to paint the kitchen. There really isn't much left to do and while I'm hesitant for all the family memories and Jenson reasons to sell, the letter I find posted through the door makes me more eager than ever to be done with it.

It's from the 'company' and I use that term loosely, who now want to collect on their debt. They want me to ring them with a progress report. Yeah, well they can wait. I stuff the letter in my handbag and throw myself into decorating.

———————

BY FRIDAY, I'm desperate for Jenson and Amelia to return. It feels like they've been away forever. Just not hearing Amelia's shouts and giggles from the garden next door is strange. I've been going in quickly each morning just to check the house is still in good repair but other than that, I've continued to hurry to complete the decorating.

The estate agent visits that afternoon. The house is ready for the market. They take photos and measurements. On Monday the house goes up for sale. I've spent the last two evenings applying for jobs up and down the country, although more of them were local to here than I want to admit to myself.

And to add to my loneliness, Carl finished yesterday, so there's been no banter with him today. He has however forced me to meet them all tonight and where are we meeting? InHale, although apparently he's been warned by Suki that if he thinks he's getting free drinks he can fuck off cos she's 'onto a good thing there'.

I WALK into the restaurant and Scott comes rushing over. "Boss know you're out on the town?" He winks. "Thought he'd have you chained up in the basement while he was away."

"We did that before he left." I throw back. Scott fans his face.

"You let me know if things don't work out there." he yells after me as I walk to the others.

"Get back in your kennel, Scott." Suki snaps at him as she walks past.

"What's up, sugar? Is it because I've not let you have a taste of this fine body?"

She rolls her eyes. "I don't care for the flavour of mutt." She gestures to a corner of the restaurant. "They're all sat over there and I've told my cousin, next time can he arrange to go out when I'm not working so I can join in the fun instead of serving it up."

"The only fun you can serve up is a fun-ghi pizza." Scott says snidely as he brings drinks to the table.

"What is going on with you two?" I ask Suki.

"He's a dickhead manwhore. Can't be doing with his type who think they're God's gift. And he can't

ANGEL DEVLIN & TRACY LORRAINE

understand why I'm not falling for his so-called charms."

I decide I might have to mention to Jenson about checking the rota so these two aren't on the same shifts too often.

I end up having a great evening once more and I'm more than a little merry when I reach my house but I change my mind and walk up the path instead into Jenson's. I crawl beneath his sheets and pull his pillow to my nose breathing him in deep. God, I miss him so much. Does he feel the same way? I need to know. I decide that when he comes home I'm going to tell him how I feel and see if the feeling is reciprocated. Then I can try to find somewhere local to live. I fall asleep and dream happy thoughts of living in Jenson's house and being Amelia's stepmum.

OF COURSE ONCE I'M sober the next morning I lay wondering what the hell I was thinking letting myself into my lover's house and sleeping in his bed like frikking Goldilocks. What a nutjob. However, while I don't have much to do today, I decide to strip the bedding off and wash it and do a few household chores so Jenson can come back to a clean and tidy home. Tidying Amelia's room, I spot a photo frame lying on its side at the back of her desk. Picking it up I gasp as I see Jenson standing next to a tall brunette. A baby Amelia is in his arms. The brunette is giving her all to the camera. The ex-wife.

She's extremely attractive on the outside, I'll give her that. Insane feelings of jealousy burn through me and I become increasingly annoyed that she had Jenson and Amelia, a gorgeous family, and she left them.

There are two sides to every story. I remind myself. You don't know why she left. I mean what would cause a woman to leave her own child?

For the first time, I get a slight pang of doubt. I really don't know Jenson that well. What will he think to me tidying his house, being around his things? Yes, he left me a key but not for snooping. I put the photo back exactly as I found it and I take the bedding with me back home.

WHEN SUNDAY MORNING COMES AROUND, I head straight for the local supermarket where I grab a copy of The Sunday Times. With the paper spread across my countertop I drink a hot coffee and read the amazing review of InHale and the interview with the 'charismatic' owner. There's an accompanying photograph of Jenson. The black and white shot shows the shadows under his cheekbones, the intensity of his gaze. He's a beautiful man. I decide to try and make my own version of a chilli sauce so that when they get home this evening I have something for us all to eat. It occupies my time.

THOUGH JENSON SENT AN 'ARRIVED SAFELY' text, I'd asked him not to text me often, but to take lots of photos and to focus on having the most amazing time with Amelia while they were away.

It's six pm when my phone dings.

Delayed at Charles de Gaulle. ETA unknown.

DISAPPOINTED, I sit back on the sofa and try to distract myself with the television although I feel like I'm watching the clock tick second by second, just waiting for another message.

It's dark outside when I remember I haven't put the bedding back on Jenson's bed and that it's still on the line in my garden. I dash outside and feel it, glad it's yet to get that damp horrible feel of an evening when the sun has gone. Throwing the pegs down on the countertop I rush next door, remake the beds and then I open a few windows a little to let some fresh air into the too warm house.

I'm sending a text as I walk back to mine asking Jenson if he's making progress so I don't realise there's a man standing outside my house until I smack right into his chest. I let out a small scream but turning my head there's no one around on the street.

"Hey, darlin'," the man drawls. He's not as tall as Jenson but he's twice as wide with muscles on muscles. It was like colliding with cement.

"W- what do y- you want?" I manage to stutter out.

"I'm from Dellaby Enterprises. Just checking on our investment." He looks me up and down and my heart thuds hard in my chest.

"The house goes up for sale tomorrow. You'll have your money soon."

"Good." He leans in closer to me. "Because otherwise we'll need to add to the invoice. I'd be happy to take payment in another way." He strokes his hand up my face. I can't move.

He laughs and begins to walk down the path.

"Be seeing you soon, darlin'."

As the guy gets in his car and drives away, I realise that while I was distracted, a taxi must have pulled up further down the street, because outside his house is Jenson with a fast-asleep Amelia in his arms.

"Well, you didn't waste much time." His eyes narrow as he shoots his venom at me.

"No." I realise what Jenson would have seen, the man with his hand down my cheek. "It's not what you—"

"Yeah, that's what my ex-wife said when I found her in the arms of our maître d'. Save it. I thought you were different." He turns to go into his house.

"Jenson, let me explain. I need your help. That was—"

"I need to get my daughter to bed. If you need help give your new boyfriend a ring." With that Jenson puts his key in the lock, opens the door and walks inside with Amelia. I watch a few minutes later as he goes back to the top of the path to collect their cases. He doesn't even look at me and then he closes his door firmly behind him. If it wasn't for Amelia, I guessed he'd have slammed it.

The reality of the last ten minutes hits me. The threats and then Jenson's mistaken assumption that I'd been seeing someone else. Tremors hit my body and I struggle to get my shaking limbs back into my house. I check the door is locked three times and then make sure every window in the house is firmly closed. I barely sleep, thinking every noise is the guy coming back. By the time dawn breaks on Monday, I know that I can't stay in this house on my own another night.

But where can I go?

17

JENSON

MY BODY VIBRATES with anger as I carry my sleeping daughter into the house. At no point did I even consider Leah would do the dirty. I was so swept away by her beauty and dirty mouth and now I feel like a total fucking fool that I didn't see it coming. I should have seen the signs. Just like I did with my ex.

Lowering Amelia to her bed, she immediately turns over and grabs onto her closest teddy.

I stand for a few minutes and allow my mind to run back over the last few days. That place really was what dreams are made of. It was everything. So much more than I expected it to be. I thought my heart was going to explode that first time we drove up towards the castle. Amelia's nose was smashed against the glass window trying to take it all in.

I was on such a high all the way home, even the delay didn't dampen my spirits. We'd had an incredible time, but now Amelia was exhausted and I was desperate to see Leah. I never could have expected to walk into what I just did. I'd even texted her to say we were in a taxi. What fucking game is she playing at?

My teeth grind and the need to break something gets too much. Dropping a kiss on Amelia's cheek, I quickly leave her room and head out for our abandoned cases.

She's still there, standing by her front door. I can feel her stare, but I refuse to look over. I will not allow her to see how much she's just ripped me apart.

I knew falling for her so damn fast would only get me in trouble, but I never thought it would be like this.

Throwing our cases down in the hallway, I close the front door behind me. What I really want to do is slam it so I feel the reverberations of my anger through my feet but with Amelia sleeping soundly above my head I can hardly do that.

So I do the next best thing. I march into the

kitchen and grab the expensive bottle of whiskey my dad bought me for Christmas a few years ago and twist the top.

The golden liquid sloshes in the glass as my hand shakes. The second I've got the bottle on the counter, I lift the tumbler to my lips and down the entire measure in one. It burns, a lot more than I ever remember it doing when I used to drink it regularly, but the second the warmth hits my stomach, I know it's exactly what I need.

"DADDY, DADDY, DADDY," Amelia squeals as the bed bounces. Rolling over, I groan, the pounding in my head increasing as I become more conscious. "Can we look at the photos now?"

"Uh..." I clear my throat when nothing but a hoarse groan comes out. "In a bit, yeah? Why don't you go and put the TV on and I'll be down soon?"

I feel her stare for a few seconds, but I refuse to open my eyes, already aware that it's too bright for me to have thought about shutting the curtains when I eventually stumbled up here last night—or early this morning.

"Daddy, are you okay?"

"Yeah, baby. Just a bit tired from chasing you around." Even the sound of my own voice makes my head hurt more. This is exactly why I don't usually drink when in charge of a child.

"We can just have a quiet day then, Daddy. I'll go and make us a den to hang out in."

"Sounds good."

It's not until she's safely downstairs that I attempt to pry my eyes open. I regret it the moment the sunlight hit my irises, but I know I can't hide in here in the dark all day, even as much as I'd like to.

I manage a quick shower and to brush my teeth before stumbling my way down the stairs. Thank fuck I had the hindsight to book today off work, although I thought I'd be struggling from exhaustion not heartbreak.

The thought of Leah with another man has pain shooting out from my chest. The faster she gets that house sold and gets the hell out of my life the better.

Kick-starting the coffee machine, I pour Amelia a milk and fix us both a bowl of cereal. The last thing I want to do right now is eat, but I can only hope it'll soak up some of last night's alcohol.

"Amelia, breakfast," I call seconds before her footsteps run this way. I've no idea how she's running around after the crazy few days we've had. She must be exhausted. Just as I think that, she comes haring around the corner dragging a blanket behind her that gets caught on the sideboard in the corner and I just about manage to catch her flying little body as she heads my way.

"Whoa, you need to slow down." Her eyes are wide as she looks up at me in shock before she nods. "I think a quiet day is definitely in order. I might even allow you to put a princess film on."

"Yesss, I know which one I want first."

First?

OUR PLANS for a quiet day last about two hours before Amelia insists that she wants to go out and play in the garden, seeing as the sun's now broken through the clouds. I manage to put an end to her idea of going to knock for Leah to see if she wants to come over for another water fight.

I'm covering her arms with suntan lotion when banging comes from outside.

"What's that, Daddy?"

Climbing to my feet, I find another man at Leah's house, only this one is hammering a 'For Sale' sign into the front lawn. The sight is like a baseball bat to the chest and I stumble back from the window.

"What's he doing?" Amelia asks innocently.

"He's putting a 'For Sale' sign in front of Leah's house."

"Is she moving?"

"Yeah she is, baby."

Amelia's chin starts to wobble. "Can't she move in here?"

Rubbing my hand over my face and up into my hair, I raise my eyes to the ceiling to pray for the answer to hit me.

"She can't, Amelia."

"But why?" she whines.

My frustration grows and I snap. "She just can't okay. Go and play outside."

Tears fill her eyes before she turns and runs from the house. The sound of her cries fills the air, making me feel like the worst dad on the planet.

Rubbing at the pain in my chest that won't abate, I watch through the open French doors as she runs right to the end of the garden and starts climbing up the ladder to her tree house.

Knowing that I need to allow us both a minute to breathe, I turn back to the coffee machine to get another mug when the worst sound in the world hits my ears. Amelia's bloodcurdling scream. Dropping the mug in my hand, it falls and shatters on the tiled floor as I turn on my heels and run towards where she is.

I run barefoot, dressed in only a pair of shorts, to the end of the garden where I can see my baby's lifeless body laid out on the wood chippings below her tree house.

"Amelia," I cry, hoping it'll be enough to bring her around, but when I get to her and fall down on my knees at her side, she's still out cold.

The tears that she was crying because I snapped at her are still wet on her cheeks.

"No," I cry. "Wake up. Wake up, please, baby."

My eyes run over her small body looking for any injuries, but I see no blood.

I run my thumb over her cheek, drying her tears and praying to whoever the fuck will listen to me that she'll open her eyes.

"It's okay, Daddy's here. Come on, just open your eyes. Show me you're o- okay." The last few words fall from my lips on a sob. I'm totally useless right now.

Then a warm hand lands on my shoulder. I didn't even hear anyone approaching.

"Ambulance, please." Just the sound of her calm,

soothing voice settles something inside me. I don't hear the rest of her conversation. I'm too lost in the relief that I'm not alone right now, and in the panic coursing around my body.

"The ambulance will be here any minute. Everything will be okay."

I can't drag my eyes away from my daughter to look at her. I'm not sure I really want to because amongst everything I'm still too angry and disappointed with her. But then her arm wraps around my shoulder and she joins me on the floor and my entire body sags in relief.

"Come on, we need to get her in the recovery position. Do you think she's hurt herself aside from bumping her head?"

"No, I... I don't think so. Fuck," I bark, standing and shoving my hands into my hair and pulling as hard as I can. "This is all my fucking fault. What have I done to her?"

"This is not your fault, Jenson. Now get back down here and support her until the experts arrive."

The wood chippings dig into my knees as I drop back down beside my daughter. Reaching out, I place my hand on her shoulder. I'm powerless but look up when Leah's delicate warm palm covers mine.

My breath catches when I take in her face because although she may sound calm right now and like she knows what she's doing, her eyes are wide in panic and she's got tears streaming down her face.

"It'll be okay," she whispers as the sound of a siren fills the air around us before paramedics run down the garden.

18

LEAH

I'D SPENT the morning sat nursing hot drinks and staring into space. I'd had hundreds of different ideas of how I could go and explain last night to Jenson. They mixed with doubts and thoughts that maybe I should just see this as a sign and move the fuck on. It's a bittersweet moment when a small white van pulls up and a guy gets out and hammers a 'For Sale' sign into the front garden. It's almost bang on the spot where Jenson found me with my injured knee.

I'm lost in my head once more when I hear a bloodcurdling scream from next door's garden. I'm out of the back door like a greyhound out of the trap, Amelia my rabbit. I jump the small fence that separates our gardens and dash for the tree house where Amelia's unconscious body lies in the wood chippings.

Jenson is unsurprisingly hysterical.

We get Amelia in the recovery position while we wait. Her breathing seems okay, thank God. I ask her to 'open her eyes' but there's no response.

I keep checking her breaths until the ambulance arrives and then Jenson and Amelia are gone. I stay behind to lock the house up, and clear pieces of broken mug and spilled coffee I find on the floor. Then I decide that whether I'm welcome at the hospital or not, I'm going. I return home, phone a cab, gather my things and then I'm on my way.

I'm directed to Jenson sitting at the side of an awake Amelia in bed.

"Oh, thank God." I cry.

"They're going to do a scan to make sure everything's okay, but it seems to be just a concussion. She has to rest and they're keeping her in overnight."

"My head hurts, Leah. I fell." Amelia says groggily.

"They've given her some painkillers." Jenson explains.

"Am I okay to be here?" I ask him.

"Don't leave me, Leah. You can talk princesses."

Amelia's small voice tears my heart wide open. I walk towards the spare seat at the side of Jenson.

I can see Jenson is trying hard to fight back tears and I know what he's thinking because I thought it too. That for one brief moment in time, the thought hit that Amelia was lying there dead. I touch his arm. "It's going to be okay." I take the seat next to him.

Amelia falls back to sleep and Jenson turns to me.

"I'm sorry about last night," he says. "We've not spoken about, well, not defined what we are, and I have no right to tell you how to spend your time."

"Jenson, you complete idiot. That man was from the company who my parents owe the money to. He was threatening me."

Jenson's eyes widen. "But I saw…"

"His hand running down my cheek. Yes, he was saying I might find another way to make a payment."

"What the…?" Jenson punches the bottom of the bed. Luckily it doesn't wake Amelia.

"Jenson!" I admonish.

"I'll kill him. Where do I find him?"

"You don't. You stay at your daughter's side where you belong. The house is up for sale now. Once they've been paid that's it. Done. Over."

"How do you know that though? I hear about

these companies and how they add interest all the time so you owe them forever."

I shrug my shoulders. "They can't take what I don't have and the debt is from my parents who are dead, so good luck with them getting any more money from anyone. And I'll probably be gone, won't I? Moved on. So hopefully this will be the end of it. Time to draw a line."

"Are you talking about the house now or us?"

"Is there an us? I don't know what you want, Jenson. It's not even a month since we met. And you have your daughter to consider."

"She adores you."

"Yeah, but how does her dad feel about me?"

Reaching for me, his fingers cup my chin gently and turn my face to his. "I think I'm falling in love with you, okay? The days in Disneyland were incredible, seeing Amelia's face, but the nights were never ending. All the time we were there Amelia kept saying what you would think as she met each princess. You've stolen pieces of both of our hearts. I do not want you to leave. I want you to stay, with us."

Holy fucking hell.

"But we barely know each other."

"I know enough. I've felt more for you in weeks than I felt for Amelia's mother all the time I knew her. Yes, we could wait, but why bother? Why not just say 'to hell with it' and take a chance? Look at today. In the blink of an eye I could have lost my daughter. I'm not living my life with any more regrets. Come live with us, Leah."

"Oh... okay."

"You will?"

I nod. "I thought I was being crazy, feeling all these huge feelings for you and Amelia; wanting to belong with you both. With what happened with my parents I also don't want to waste a moment of life. It's too short."

Jenson reaches over to me, pulling his chair towards mine and his lips meet my own.

"That's just a taster of what I'm going to do to you later." He picks up his phone. "Now, just excuse me a minute."

I listen as he calls the estate agency and puts in an offer on my home for the asking price.

"What are you doing?" I mouth, but he just waves me away.

I laugh as my own phone rings and I ask them to hold.

"Jenson, what are you doing? I can't ask you to do this."

"It's not for you. It's for us. I'm going to make the

houses one large detached. I don't want neighbours and given the restaurant is booked for two years ahead now thanks to the piece in The Sunday Times, I can well afford it."

Smiling, I return to my phone. "I'll accept the offer."

Once I've said goodbye to the estate agent, Jenson grabs my hand. "I shall make sure that loan company is well out of your hair too." I see a tic in his cheek and a flash of fire in his eyes. "I didn't get to be where I am in business without having a couple of people in my pocket who can deal with arseholes."

We sit by Amelia's bedside, chatting and holding hands, taking turns to fetch coffees and sandwiches etc until the hospital decide Amelia is okay to be taken home after all, with 24-hour observation. We take it in turns to sit by her bedside all night.

WE SPEND A QUIET DAY TOGETHER. Amelia is recovering well in that way kids do and greets the news I'm moving in with screams and whoops of delight. I fix her pancakes for tea because that's what she wants and I don't give a shit. She just had an injury, she can have them for breakfast, lunch, and dinner right now, and once she's bathed and in bed, I tell Jenson to take a seat at the dinner table while I warm up the chilli sauce I made a couple of days ago.

I'm excited for him to try out my cooking. I've never been able to so much as boil an egg and I'm keen to learn.

Sat near each other we both take our first mouthful of sauce. My face soon turns beet red and I watch as Jenson runs for the sink and swallows a glass full of water.

"How much chilli did you put in it?" he asks.

I can't answer. My whole body is on fire. Obviously, too much.

Jenson has the milk out of the fridge. He takes a huge gulp straight from the carton and then passes it to me. I'm burning up. I begin stripping off because I have to get cool somehow. My whole body is sweating.

Jenson isn't half as affected as I am judging by the fact that his hands are roaming my now naked body.

"Jenson." I gasp. "I'm freaking melting."

"Yup, hot stuff." He strips off his own clothes and picking me up he lifts me onto the kitchen table, pulling off my panties and standing between my thighs.

"Don't you dare put your mouth on me. I don't want my pussy on fire."

"Oh it's gonna be on fire all right," he says and he pushes into me.

I groan.

"See, Leah. Look at how kind I am. Distracting you from the fire in your mouth by putting it somewhere else." He thrusts hard, and harder still.

We fuck at the dining table while chilli sweat mingles with sexy and I know that I am so hot for this man it's ridiculous.

EPILOGUE

Jenson

Two Months Later...

LEAH MOVED in the day we got back from the hospital with Amelia. It was obvious that I'd jumped to conclusions about what was going on with the guy I found her with when I returned from Paris, but what I hadn't appreciated was the impact he had on Leah.

I didn't think anything of it when she first asked me to go next door with her to grab some of her stuff, but as she lifted her arm to slide the key into the lock, her hand was trembling.

"Are you okay?" I asked.

"Of course." Her eyes darted into each room as we walked towards the stairs.

"Leah, what's wrong?"

"That guy, the one you saw. It's crazy, I know, but I just got the idea he'd come back and..." a shudder ran through her body.

"Hey, it's okay." Reaching out I pulled her trembling body against mine. "It'll be sorted in a few weeks, but in the meantime, you don't need to come back in here. I'll get everything you need and you'll be safe next door with us."

Glancing up, she stared into my eyes. In that moment I knew that what we were doing was right. The two of us were meant to be.

AS PROMISED, Leah didn't step foot back in that house until it was in my name and the loan shark had been paid off. But even then, it wasn't until Carl and his mate smashed through the wall to connect the two houses ready to create the kind of kitchen I've only been able to dream of that gave it closure.

It's by far taking the biggest chunk of our renovation budget but Leah refused to have it any other way. She insisted we needed plenty of space so I could continue attempting to teach her how to cook, but more importantly, we needed a huge, sturdy kitchen table in the centre for other activities we like to take part in in the middle of the kitchen.

"Hey, what are you thinking about?" A delicate pair of hands slip around my sides and find their way under my t-shirt so she can trace the lines of my abs with her fingertips.

"Just imagining all the surfaces I can fuck you on when this room's finished."

"Hmmm." Reaching up on her tiptoes, her lips find the exposed skin of my neck and she trails kisses along the hem of my shirt. "Anything would be better than the concrete floor we've got at the moment."

"You know for a fact that wouldn't stop me."

Her cheeks heat as memories hit her. Seeing as we live with a nosy six-year-old, getting some alone time can be somewhat of a challenge, but we've been creative when needs be and have christened every room in my house. Now we've opened up into next door we've got a whole lot of new rooms to experiment in.

"It's so weird school being back and not having Amelia here."

"I know but you know what that means?" Leah's eyebrow quirks up in question. "We can paint naked."

Pulling her around to my front, I take in her paint covered vest and tiny shorts that I always loved so much.

"Hmmm, I could get on board with naked painting." Her eyes roam over my body as if I'm already naked and my cock swells. It might have only been hours since I had her last but it's never enough. I'm obsessed with my girl and I can't see that changing anytime soon.

Stalking towards her, she has no choice but to back up to exactly where I want her.

"Do you know where we're standing?"

She glances around, her brows drawing together. "Uh... in the kitchen?"

"Yeah, that much is kinda obvious, but no, I mean here. This exact spot."

"You're being weird."

My heart begins to race knowing that my well-planned moment is about to happen. I can only hope it plays out exactly as I've imagined a million times over.

Taking her hand in mine, I lift it to my lips and kiss her knuckles.

"Jenson, what are you doing?"

"This spot right here is exactly where you sat the morning we met. You were perched right here on a chair wearing those exact damn shorts and a vest that barely covered your tits much like you are now." My eyes flick down briefly to her paint speckled breasts and I lick my lips before continuing. "This spot is where I put my hands on you for the first time and experienced the shock that still shoots around my body now when I touch you."

Leah sucks her bottom lip into her mouth and chews as she listens to what I've got to say, desperate to know where the hell I'm going with this.

"It's something I want to feel for the rest of my life." Squeezing her hand a little tighter, I drop to my knee, her gasp breaking through the sounds of my blood racing past my ears. "Leah Ward, will you allow me to feel that way for the rest of my life and agree to be my wife?"

"Jenson," she whispers from behind the hand covering her gaping mouth. "Are you serious?"

Digging my hand into my pocket, I pull out the box that I realise I probably should have had in my hand a few minutes ago.

Flipping the lid open, I hold out the simple platinum solitaire diamond out for her to see. "Deadly serious. Will you be my wife, Leah?"

"Yes, yes, yes," she squeals dropping down to her knees with me.

Pulling the ring from its cushion, I take her trembling hand in mine and slide her new piece of jewellery up her finger.

"Oh my god," she whispers as she wiggles her fingers, making the diamond sparkle in the spotlights shining down on us. "I'm going to be Mrs Hale."

Leaning over her, I force her to lay back onto the dusty concrete floor. Settling between her legs, I take her cheeks in my hands. "Leah Hale has a good ring to it, don't you think?"

Her response is just a moan as her heels dig into my arse, pressing my length against her core. "I think we need some more practice if you're going to make an honest woman out of me."

"My pleasure, baby. My pleasure."

Leah
One year later

THE MAKE-UP ARTIST has finished my make-up (and put some gloss on Amelia's lips at her insistence), the hair stylist has done both mine and Amelia's hair in soft waves, and we stand in mine and Jenson's bedroom looking at our reflections.

"We look like the prettiest princesses that there ever were." Amelia grins, touching her tiara. "Now come on and marry my daddy so I can give you my wedding present because I'm BURSTING."

I laugh and we make our way carefully downstairs where I'm greeted in the doorway by Carl. It seems crazy to think that the man who will take my father's place walking me down the aisle is the giant bear of a man who came to my door a little over a year ago to help renovate my parents' old house. He's become such a good friend to me and to Jenson and the daft sod cried when I asked him. He's looking a little teary now.

"Do not start, because if you ruin my make-up I will end you." I warn him.

"You both look so beautiful. It's an honour to escort you to the service."

There is ice sparkling on the ground like a dazzling white carpet, and a crispness to the air, but it has stayed rain free with clear skies and that's all I could ask for. The limo takes me to the hotel where my groom awaits.

As I walk towards Jenson, sweet music playing, he stares at me and mouths, "I love you."

We stand side by side making our vows and then the officiant announces the moment I've been desperate for. Jenson's kiss holds everything in it, with promises for the future, but I already have everything I need and more.

We have a meal with Jenson's family and with our close friends. His parents are fabulous though they live so far away we don't see them that often. I hope that when my children have children, I'm close enough to be a huge part of their lives.

Yes, my children. Plural. I am adopting Amelia and neither of them know it but there's another little person growing in my tummy right now.

We arrive home and Amelia grabs my hand. "Can I do it now, Daddy, please? I waited all the damn day."

I snigger as Jenson's eyes roll. "What is it, cupcake?" I ask her.

"Well, I know you're gonna adopt me to be my mummy, but I want you to know that you already are. I'm not calling you Leah anymore. Nuh-uh. I love you, Mummy."

Tears roll down my face as I clutch this sweet girl. "I love you too, Amelia. And guess what?" I look from Amelia to my husband. "So does the baby brother or sister I have growing inside my tummy."

"Whaaaattt?" she screams. "Oh my god, oh my god. I'm gonna be a big sister." Then she bursts into tears. Jenson sweeps me into his arms and kisses me hard, placing his hand on my tummy.

"Really? Our baby is growing in there?"

"Really." I nod.

We gather Amelia in a hug and ask if she's okay. She rubs her eyes and says. "I'm just so bloody happy."

"I'll be talking to you about your language later, young lady." Jenson scolds. "But on this occasion I'd just like to say I'm just so bloody happy too."

We stand in a family hug in our family home and I just know that somewhere my parents also have a tear of happiness in their eyes.

Because I came home and found home.

THE END

Read Kaylie's story next in Baby Daddy Rescue.
https://books2read.com/u/bPQWgR

Read on for a sneak peek!

BABY DADDY RESCUE SNEAK PEEK

Chapter One
Kaylie

As I burst in through the door, the other ladies in the bathroom all turn to look at me. Sympathy flashes across a few faces. That means they've either seen, or worse, smelled my date.

I'm burned by online dates almost every date, yet my desperation to find the one still keeps me coming back.

Dropping down onto the closed toilet seat, I suck in some clean, albeit bathroom air, and pull my phone from my bag. It's been vibrating on my lap for the last few minutes as if even my phone knows this is my most disastrous date out of all the horrendous ones that have gone before.

I almost sigh when I see my best friend's name appear on my screen. He seems to always know just when I need him.

Aiden: How's it going?

Me: Fucking disaster. I'm surprised you can't smell him from wherever you are.

I add the little throwing up emoji and hit send, expecting a handful of laughing gifs back.

Aiden: Want me to come rescue you?

My heart swells knowing that he'd ditch whatever he's doing tonight--probably some unsuspecting female who's about to get fucked and chucked faster than she can blink.

Me: No, it's fine. I've got this.

What I need is a knight in shining fucking armour to sweep me away and do all sorts of wicked things to me. I don't need to force Aiden away from adding another notch on his bedpost.

I take my time washing my hands and spray a little extra perfume across my body, hoping that it might cover up my date's putrid stench.

Plastering a smile on my face, I head back out. He might be all kinds of wrong for me, but I'm also not a heartless bitch and I couldn't walk out the moment I arrived. I just don't have it in me. All I can hope now is that he pays for the meal so at least I can say I had some free food, even if it was all tainted by his smell.

"There you are. I thought maybe you'd fallen in."

Sadly not.

"Sorry, there was a queue." Mark glances around the half empty restaurant but he doesn't say anything.

"I hope you don't mind but I've ordered our desserts."

"Oh... uh..."

"Apple pie all around. It's been too long since Mummy made it for me."

Raising an eyebrow, I don't ask because he's already explained more than once in our hour of being here about how he still lives with his mother and has no intentions of moving out any time soon while she still does everything for him. *Shame she doesn't make him shower.*

"I don't actually like—"

My words are cut off when two bowls are placed in front of us.

"Enjoy." The waiter is different to the others we've had all night and as I look up, I can see why. The others are all huddled in the corner laughing. I'm glad my Friday night misery is entertaining them. And I haven't even got the melt-in-the-middle chocolate pudding I spied when ordering. I bloody love chocolate. I hate apples.

"Mmm... so good," Mark mumbles, little bits of pie flying from his mouth, making me want to puke in mine.

I pick at the vanilla ice cream that's sitting on the side but mostly I just watch it melt. That is until a very familiar voice fills my ears and has my spine straightening.

"What the hell do you think you're doing?"

Running my eyes up Aiden's tall and lean body, I can't help but note every difference to the man sitting opposite me.

"I'm sorry, do you mind? I'm on a date."

"Yeah with my girlfriend. Care to explain why?"

Aiden leans in. I see the exact moment he regrets it because his cheeks puff out as if he's gagging.

"I'm... I'm sorry... She was on..."

"I don't care." Turning his amused, although slightly repulsed eyes to me, he can't help but notice the almost full bowl sitting in front of me. "Come on, baby. Let's get you home. You're in for a spanking tonight."

Mark splutters before Aiden's giant hand wraps around my upper arm and I'm pulled so I'm standing right in front of him.

"And you wore my favourite dress. You know what that thing does to me." He growls, actually fucking growls like a wild animal as he puts on a great show of checking mc out.

Chancing a glance at Mark, I note he looks like he's about to shit his pants any minute. Although from the smell permeating the air we could argue that he already has.

DOWNLOAD NOW to discover the rest of Kaylie and Aiden's story.

ABOUT ANGEL DEVLIN

Angel Devlin writes stories as hot as her coffee. She lives in Sheffield with her partner, son, and a gorgeous whippet called Bella.

Newsletter:
Sign up here for Angel's latest news and exclusive content.
https://geni.us/angeldevlinnewsletter

ABOUT TRACY LORRAINE

Tracy Lorraine is a new adult and contemporary romance author. Tracy is in her thirties and lives in a cute Cotswold village in England with her husband and daughter. Having always been a bookaholic with her head stuck in her Kindle, Tracy decided to try her hand at a story idea she dreamt up and hasn't looked back since.

Be the first to find out about new releases and offers. Sign up to my newsletter here.

If you want to know what I'm up to and see teasers and snippets of what I'm working on, then you need to be in my Facebook group. Join Tracy's Angels here.

Keep up to date with Tracy's books at
www.tracylorraine.com

Printed in Great Britain
by Amazon

42952339R00128